The name couldn't have been more fitting. With his hair tousled around his face, he could have been one of the bandits that once roamed and pillaged this wild country.

"Do you want me to leave?" Maggie asked. It was frightening to admit to herself just how much she wanted to stay.

"No, I still need someone, but you may not want to live by my standards. In two more days you may be crying for New York. You have noticed there *is* a big difference?"

"I would be blind not to have noticed," she replied.

"And you still want to stay?"

Did she? Did she really want to stay and take the chance of having her heart twisted out of shape?

"Yes," she decided.

Dear Reader,

Welcome to Silhouette. Experience the magic of the wonderful world where two people fall in love. Meet heroines who will make you cheer for their happiness, and heroes (be they the boy next door or a handsome, mysterious stranger) who will win your heart. Silhouette Romances reflect the magic of love—sweeping you away with books that will make you laugh and cry, heartwarming, poignant stories that will move you time and time again.

In the next few months, we're publishing romances by many of your all-time favorites, such as Diana Palmer, Brittany Young, Emilie Richards and Arlene James. Your response to these authors and other authors of Silhouette Romances has served as a touchstone for us, and we're pleased to bring you more books with Silhouette's distinctive medley of charm, wit and—above all—*romance*.

I hope you enjoy this book and the many stories to come. Experience the magic!

Sincerely,

Tara Hughes
Senior Editor
Silhouette Books

STELLA BAGWELL
Moonlight Bandit

Silhouette Romance

Published by Silhouette Books New York

America's Publisher of Contemporary Romance

To my mother and stepfather, Lucille and Wayne,
for first showing Amarillo to me, and
for all their love and encouragement.

SILHOUETTE BOOKS
300 E. 42nd St., New York, N.Y. 10017

ISBN: 0-373-08485-4

First Silhouette Books printing February 1987

America's Publisher of Contemporary Romance

Printed in the U.S.A.

STELLA BAGWELL

is a small-town girl and an incurable romantic—a combination she feels enhances her writing. When she isn't at her typewriter she enjoys reading, listening to music, sketching pencil drawings and sewing her own clothes. Most of all she enjoys exploring the outdoors with her husband and young son.

Chapter One

Maggie Winslow pushed back the dark sunglasses to their proper position on the bridge of her nose with a tired sigh. The glasses would surely slide down in a matter of minutes; it was inevitable when every inch of her body was bathed in sweat.

She wished she could take the infernal things off and throw them out the window, but that would hardly be a wise move. They were the only protection she had against the glaringly bright sunshine, and her eyes were already burning from all the driving she'd done this past week.

The Texas Panhandle! She just couldn't believe it! Western Oklahoma had been bad enough. But this! From behind the dark glasses, her eyes roamed the monotonous rolling plains. There was nothing here! Nothing but dry yellow grass, cows and the occasional derrick of an oil well being drilled.

She must have been insane to think she actually wanted to come out here, she thought disgruntledly. Maybe she should have taken her mother's advice and consulted an analyst before she set out on this trip, she thought with a bit of sour humor.

This place was unbearably dry, barren and ugly. The land was so flat and endless that it merged into the sky, making it difficult to tell just where one started and the other ended. It looked to Maggie as if she was driving into a haze of sheer nothing!

If this was the Texas she'd heard boasted about, then she hated to think what the rest of the state was like. Surely God had forgotten to wave his hand over this place when He'd created Earth. She couldn't see how He would have left it this way purposely. Why, even the few trees that were scattered around were all bent into crippled arcs facing north, their leaves wind whipped and scraggly. They were proof of the strength of the West Texas winds and she wondered if the wind ever stopped blowing, if the people who were crazy enough to live out here were as permanently bent as all the trees seemed to be.

One thing she did know: her arms were literally aching from fighting the wind to keep the Alfa Romeo on the highway and she knew that if she had to go much farther, she would simply burst into tears.

This was totally unlike Maggie. She had been in many difficult situations and places all over the world. None of them had shaken her headstrong spirit or determination. But this place was hideous, she thought despairingly as she slipped a hand between her neck and the heavy swathe of honey-blond hair. Certainly her extremely successful career as a model had never led her to any place like West Texas. For once she was overwhelmed.

When Maggie had first announced she was going to Amarillo, everyone back in New York City had declared her insane. Especially her modeling agent, Phillip Saville. At first he'd been incredulous and later furious when he realized she wouldn't change her plans.

Her thoughts whirled back to the night before she had left on this journey. Phillip had taken her to an exclusive French restaurant for dinner, and she had worn a daring evening gown of pink lamé and enormous golden earrings.

Phillip had told her she looked ravishing, but the compliment failed to inspire her. In her line of work she was constantly getting compliments. So many, in fact, that she often wondered if they were given sincerely. Did people really think she was beautiful, or were they merely saying that because she was successful?

Many people thought Maggie's poise and cool confidence came from the beauty she possessed. They thought all she had to do was smile and the door to success was instantly opened.

Because she had worked hard for her career, reactions that belittled her efforts infuriated Maggie. And between her stints as a model, she had gone to college and pursued a degree in business management. She had a brain and she could use it. Maybe this had partially been the reason she had remained unmoved against Phillip's persuasions that night. He often forgot that she possessed a keen mind.

"Maggie, do you realize what this will do to your career?" Phillip had demanded. "It's June. The fall fashions are already being designed. If you're not here to work—" He left the sentence unfinished as his blue eyes pleaded with her. "Dear Maggie, there's a row of young lovelies just dying to take your place—if you're away and unavailable, they will."

"That's a chance I'll have to take," Maggie answered as she sipped the dry white wine. The diamonds on her fingers glittered in the candlelight as she replaced the stemmed crystal goblet.

Across the richly laid table, Phillip Saville frowned impatiently. He was a handsome man. In his early forties, he was tall and lean with tawny brown hair clipped in an elegant, fashionable style. But then everything about Phillip was fashionable. He made sure it was. After all, he was in the fashion business.

"Right now you're at the peak. You're such a recognizable figure that people refer to you as 'Maggie'—it's phenomenal! No one in her right mind would put a career like yours in jeopardy over some foolish whim—some idiotic inheritance from an uncle you haven't seen since you were sixteen years old!"

She nodded at the last part of his statement, a frown creasing her lovely features. "Yes, it's been nine years since I've last seen Uncle George. And I regret that; I really do," she truthfully confessed.

Phillip gave a disgruntled snort. "Then you couldn't have been very close to him. Why did he leave the property to you in the first place?"

Maggie poked at the well-prepared gourmet food with a sudden restlessness. The hushed atmosphere of the restaurant was stifling and so was Phillip's persistence. "George had no one. He never married. And his relationship with my father was so strained that he didn't leave him a dime."

"Tomas has always seemed like an amiable person. I don't understand why their relationship was strained. After all, they were brothers," Phillip reasoned with businesslike logic.

Maggie shook her head, her long fingernail tracing the edge of her wineglass. "You don't know my father. When it comes to his banking business, he can be a real monster. George was in partnership with him at one time, and they quarreled constantly. He thought Father's badgering business tactics were unnecessary and ruthless. After some years of disagreement, George sold his shares and moved to Texas. I think he was disillusioned with the whole lot—the fast city life, the money, the underhanded business deals."

Without warning, there was a prickling of tears at the back of her eyes as she remembered her gentle uncle, his rotund shape, the partially bald head and crinkling, humor-filled eyes. She'd adored him and perhaps had in some ways even been closer to him than her own father. When Maggie was small, her father was dedicated to building a banking empire. He'd had little time for Maggie or her mother. But George had made the time. And whenever there was a school function Tomas Winslow could not attend, George was always there. So much so that eventually her friends labeled him her "other father."

Although they'd continued to keep in touch through letters and phone calls, she had missed Uncle George terribly when he had moved to Texas. In the past few years, his letters had grown few and far between. But Maggie's travels as a model made it difficult for his letters to catch up to her. She supposed he'd probably gotten tired of waiting for her replies.

"You know, one of the last things he wrote to me was, 'Maggie dear, you're living in a vacuum and you don't even know it.'" Her aqua blue eyes met Phillip's with conviction. "It made me angry when I read that, and do you know why?"

"No," Phillip sighed on a bored note. He couldn't really have cared less what a disheartened relative had once said to Maggie. He just wanted to hear her say she was going to stay in New York.

"Because I knew it was the truth. And now it is something I intend to change."

Phillip's aquiline features expressed impatience. "I can't see how a few acres in the southwest could have a positive impact on your life. And if you were thinking clearly, you would agree. Texas! Good Lord, Maggie, I can't imagine you living out there among a bunch of uncouth cowboys and Mexicans. There's absolutely nothing there that could interest you. No fine arts, no fashion, no—" He broke off impatiently as Maggie's expression grew defensive.

"Uncle George was not an ignorant man," she argued. "He could speak six languages fluently, and there were very few countries he hadn't traveled through. Besides serving as a colonel in the air force during World War II, he was also a very successful businessman. He loved the ballet, Broadway, gourmet food and classical literature. There was something that kept him in West Texas."

Seeing he'd offended her, Phillip shook his head, a patronizing little smile on his face. "I wasn't referring to your uncle—"

Maggie glared at him as she took in the smooth features of his face. Phillip was a wizard at running a modeling agency, but he could be a real snob.

"Please Phillip. Don't try to change my mind."

"All right," he said angrily, losing all patience. "I'm telling you flat out. You're making a drastic mistake by deserting your work. The best thing you could do is let your lawyer turn your uncle's land over to a real estate agency."

Maggie shifted restlessly. Phillip wasn't trying to advise her. He was giving her an edict, and she resented it furiously. He was her agent, but that didn't give him the right to act as though she lacked the ability to make decisions on her own.

"Maybe I will sell the land," she replied sternly. "But not until I've seen it for myself, not until I've found what made Uncle George so happy out there. I owe him that much."

"But . . . but you make it sound like an indefinite amount of time," Phillip spluttered, aghast.

She nodded. "That's right. I haven't had a vacation in a long time. I'm well overdue for one, so I'm taking it now."

On that announcement, the topic was dropped until later that night when Phillip pulled his Mercedes to a stop in front of Maggie's brownstone apartment and was walking her safely to the door.

As she handed him the key, he pulled her into his arms. She wasn't surprised by his actions; she knew his reputation. Angry, she twisted her head to the side as he searched for her lips.

"I don't want you to leave, Maggie," he pleaded, irritated that she refused to respond to him. "And you know it's not merely because of business. I've fallen in love with you."

Maggie's soft sigh drifted away in the darkness. "Phillip, you've fallen in love with a dozen different girls since I've known you. It wasn't real then; it isn't now. You've worked with me so long that you've just grown attached to me."

"Attached?" he mused, his hands closing around her waist. "Oh, yes, that too. I guess I've always been too damned attached to you. From the first day you walked into my office with your electric blue eyes and a mane of wheat-blond hair, I've known that we belonged together."

Maggie's lips pursed with hopelessness. Phillip *had* always made his personal interest in her more than obvious. Yet they'd never gotten closer than casual dates. Maggie hadn't allowed it. She'd learned better than to get involved with a business associate. It had happened once before, a long time ago, and she had been badly burned. It had taught her a lesson about men, about herself, but not about love. God forbid that that brief entanglement could have been a taste of love. But even if she discounted the past, Phillip Saville was not a man she would ever want to get involved with. He was a taker, and she'd had enough takers to last her a lifetime.

"And when another discovery comes along, you'll feel the same way about her," Maggie said, knowing it was the truth.

He gave her a little shake. "I've had plenty of beauties walk through my door. They can't compare with you."

Maggie sighed and made an effort to pull away from him. "You're wasting your time, Phillip."

His features grew taut. "Yes, and all because of that damned Mario. That's one assignment I wish I'd never given you. Even if it did bring in half a million."

"It's not that—"

"Oh, yes, Maggie, my sweet. Ever since that fling with him you look at all men as if they were monsters," he snapped, his soft, manicured hands trying to draw her back into his arms.

His efforts repulsed Maggie and she jerked away from him impatiently, grabbed the key from his fingers and began to unlock the door herself.

"I'm going to Texas, Phillip. Nothing is going to stop me. We'll talk when I get back." She stepped over the threshold with no intentions of inviting him in for a nightcap.

He was furiously desperate as she started to close the door. "And when will you be back Maggie? When you get tired of trying to escape from the real world?" he flung at her.

"I don't know, Phillip. I just don't know," she answered truthfully, shutting the door between them.

Maggie's thoughts returned to the present, and she actually laughed out loud as her hand lifted from the steering wheel to touch her sore, sunburned shoulders. She wasn't heading for an escape; she appeared to be driving right into hell!

Thirty minutes later, Maggie breathed a sigh of relief as the outline of Amarillo came into view. She studied it against the hazy sky, wondering why someone had ever started a town out in the middle of nowhere. It seemed very strange to see a huge, thriving metropolis set out on an open plain.

There was no problem driving through the city traffic. I-40 ran right through the city and its four lanes kept the traffic flowing freely. From the directions Mr. Sanderson, George's lawyer, had given her, she was to go approximately seven miles west of the city then turn north off the interstate onto a small graveled road. There would be a gas station at the turnoff.

Well, Mr. Sanderson, I hope you've given me the right directions, Maggie thought, as she watched the major part of the city disappear behind her.

A few minutes later, she sighted the gas station. It was an ancient-looking one, probably constructed back when bloody Route 66 was built. The interstate had taken the place of the infamous highway, but apparently the gas station had managed to survive.

Maggie geared down the Alfa Romeo to make the turn, and as she did, she noticed that several dusty vehicles were parked around the station. On impulse, she decided to stop. Hopefully, the attendant could tell her if she was on the right road.

A hefty Mexican was pumping gas into a dented and scraped Nissan pickup. Maggie wanted to laugh at the sight of him cleaning the windshield with meticulous care. Phillip's Mercedes had probably never been subjected to such reverent treatment, and she wished her agent could see this, too.

There were several men sitting around the front door of the station in straight-backed, cane-bottomed chairs. They didn't appear to be customers or workers, merely loafers drinking beer and smoking cigarettes.

Now this is progress in the making, Maggie thought humorlessly as she got out of the little car and slammed the door behind her. Several pairs of male eyes followed Maggie's tall, willowly figure in yellow jogging shorts and matching tank top as she walked toward the Mexican. A yellow sweatband twisted with gold circled her forehead and kept the long strands of curly blond hair from falling in her eyes. However, the gusts of wind insisted on blowing it into her face, forcing her to hold it down with both hands.

The chubby Mexican, somewhere in his late forties, smiled warmly at her, then pointed toward the door of the station.

"The key inside the door, the bathroom around back. Should be plenty of paper," he told her in broken English.

For the first time in a long while, Maggie blushed. "I beg your pardon?" she stuttered.

"You no need bathroom?" he asked, pulling the gas nozzle out of the Nissan.

"No, I—" She stopped as he turned to place the nozzle back on the pump. She was not accustomed to having people ignore her while she was speaking. She waited a little impatiently for him to turn back to her, so when instead he started checking the oil in the Nissan, Maggie had no choice but to follow him.

"I really need some directions," she said, leaning her head a little under the hood so that he could hear her.

"If I know where you goin', *señorita*, then I tell you," he responded.

Maggie took a deep breath. "I'm looking for the Winslow farm. I was told it's not far from here."

"You won't find him there, *niña*" the man replied. Maggie thought she caught a note of sadness in his voice.

"I know that. I'm here to see about the property," she informed him.

"Oh," he grunted and pulled his head out from under the hood to point a short, stubby finger toward the north.

"Keep on this road till you cross the section line road, then turn left. About three miles, you see a trailer house, the next house was old George's. You know George from somewhere?" he asked, his interest sparked now that he knew she wasn't headed on down the interstate.

Maggie opened her mouth to answer, but a deep male voice interrupted her.

"Tony, the money for Nugget's candy and pop is on the counter," the man said to the Mexican.

Maggie turned around. Just for a second, her gaze encountered a pair of warm, tawny brown eyes. The glance only lasted a few moments, but even in that limited amount of time, she registered almost everything about him.

The man's curly dark brown hair stuck out at unruly intervals beneath a billed cap sporting a company emblem, and his darkly tanned skin contrasted with his teeth. Deep laughter lines formed from the ends of a thick sable walrus mustache when he smiled.

A little girl stood closely by his side. She appeared to be somewhere around eight years old with straight blond hair that was combed back neatly and kept in place by little red barrettes. She was popping M&Ms in her mouth with obvious relish and washing them down with orange-flavored soda pop.

She grinned at Maggie, showing a new set of front teeth. They were straight and white, and Maggie wondered how long they would stay that way if her daddy kept allowing her to partake of such sweet treats. He probably spoiled her as soon as they got out of the mother's sight, and Maggie felt a sudden squashing of her spirit as she realized that this raw-looking male was already taken.

"*Gracias*, R.J. *Hasta luego,*" Tony replied.

The man called R.J. lifted a hand in farewell, and Maggie watched out of the corner of her eye as he and the little girl walked toward the open-top army jeep. Maggie's gaze slid discreetly over the lean body dressed in Levi's and khaki shirt. There was something about him that sparked the baser side of her female instincts. Reluctantly, she recognized the feeling and wondered why, after such a long, long time, an ordinary stranger was bringing it back to her.

Maybe it was because she'd seen so many fanatical body builders and jogging nuts that this naturally well-made man was unique, even if his appearance as a whole was rather unrefined.

Once at the jeep, the man lifted the child up into the passenger seat while she carefully clutched her candy and pop, then swung himself behind the wheel.

Before he started the motor, the little girl looked up at him and said something, and he responded by leaning down and saying something in her ear. Giggling, she glanced back at Maggie and the Mexican and gave them a little wave.

Maggie had the most distinct feeling that the man's remark had been aimed at herself, and she glared at the man's back as he whipped the dusty jeep out onto the gravel road and headed east on the interstate toward Amarillo.

"You knew George?" the man called Tony asked once again.

Maggie turned back to the Mexican, angry with herself for letting some uncouth stranger distract her.

"Yes, he was my uncle. He willed his farm to me."

The man slicked back his straight black hair and grabbed Maggie's hand, pumping it furiously, then patted her on the shoulder as if she were an old, dear friend. A wide smile parted his mouth as he said, "Oh this is good, *señorita. Bueno, muy bueno.* George was *mi amigo.* He was good man. I miss him. Miss him bad. But now you here to take his place. *Es bueno,*" he boomed heartily, his black eyes beaming at her.

"Thank you," Maggie said demurely, wondering why it made her feel good to have this man welcome her.

"You can have credit anytime, *señorita*—er, what's your name?" he asked.

"Maggie," she smiled. "Maggie Winslow."

"Maggie," he repeated with a laugh, "You have all the credit you want. Groceries, gas, beer—all you want." He turned and motioned toward her little Alfa Romeo. "Pull your car over here and I fill the tank—no charge."

"Oh, no—" Maggie started, shocked at the gesture. Clearly this man was not well enough off to be giving gas away.

"*Sí, sí,*" he insisted. "For George, *mi amigo;* I do it for him."

It was a good thirty minutes before Maggie pulled away from the old station, but not before Tony had filled her tank and checked her car. He proudly introduced her to the men sitting in the shade of the building, then took her inside and rounded up a sack full of groceries for her.

The sack was sitting on the seat beside her now as she traveled slowly down the gravel road, and Tony's words came back to her.

"You take them, Maggie, then after you get moved in, you come back and visit Tony. You can pay me then."

How odd, she thought. Back home there wasn't one store in her neighborhood that would have done such a thing. True, it probably didn't amount to more than a few dollars, but it would mean a lot to someone like Tony, who worked hard for what he had. And he had done it because George was his friend.

She thought back to the men in New York City who had allegedly once been friends of George's and gave a cynical little laugh. If she had gone to one of them for a loan, they wouldn't have thought of George. The only thing interesting them would have been the collateral.

A few minutes later, Maggie was shocked once more when she pulled up to George's, or now more rightly, *her* house. It was bare and ugly. Those were the only two words to describe it.

It was a plain, rectangle shape, the outside being a dirty cream-colored stucco. There were a few windows to break the monotony, but there weren't any shutters or any kind of decorations to adorn the starkness. To add to this, there were no flowers or shrubs, only one scraggly-looking tree behind the house, and of course, it was bent toward the north. Its limbs reminded Maggie of arthritic fingers, deformed and permanently crippled.

She sighed, her tiredness tugging at her once more as she slowly climbed from the car. She had to admit that her disappointment was partially her own fault. She had built up the place in her mind as one of those beautiful, hacienda-type ranch houses. George had always possessed good taste in things, especially his luxurious home back in New York, so naturally she'd expected something nice.

For the life of her, she couldn't imagine her beloved uncle living in this house, on this dry barren land and liking it. But this had to be the right place. The mailbox out by the road said so.

Before unlocking the house, she walked around the yard, or at least what was supposed to have been a yard. The grass, or the few sprigs she could find, were a weak yellow-green while the remainder was weeds and sandburrs, one of which found its way between her heel and the sole of her sandal.

Cursing, she lifted her foot and pulled the spiky object out of her flesh. Absently rubbing the sore spot with her forefinger, she studied the horizon around her. About a quarter mile up the road was another house. It was stucco, also, but that is where the similarity ended. Even from this distance she could tell the lawn was beautifully landscaped with century plants and choya cactus, lush green grass and huge cottonwood trees.

There was a brilliant glitter of blue in the backyard of that house that looked suspiciously like a swimming pool. At least George's neighbors lived with a little luxury! Farther beyond the house was a big red barn, and in the pasture next to it were five horses, two of them colts.

Behind George's, or rather her house, there was also a big tin barn and a corral extending from one side of it. Close to it was a windmill and a watertank. It made a cranking noise as the hot gusts of wind whirled the blades around. The noise seemed loud to Maggie since there was no traffic, no people, no nothing to drown it out.

From his letters, she knew that George had once owned a few cattle, but she guessed that he had sold them off as his health began to fail. He had tried his hand at farming, too, but she could see no signs of where any crops had ever grown.

As she made her way back to the front of the house, Maggie could only think how many millions of miles away it seemed from the fantasy world of high fashion. She had always lived in a contrived environment. How was she going to endure this long enough to be able to go back to New York without having Phillip and everyone else say I told you so?

No, she thought determinedly as she stuck the key in the lock, she'd rather face this isolated desert than go back to New York where she was finding it an effort to make herself get out of bed in the morning. Phillip had been smothering her, and the modeling career she'd once loved now seemed to be lacking something.

George had once said only a person who liked himself could live out here. She had wondered what he meant at the time. Now she was beginning to see. Except for the land, there was nothing here.

Did she like herself? She had been so busy these past few years making a fortune that she didn't even know who she really was, or even if she liked the person she had become.

So was she crazy to think she might find peace of mind in this alien land? Right at the moment, it certainly seemed so.

Chapter Two

Maggie stood inside the main room of the house, her eyes slowly circling the barren walls. It was hideous!

There wasn't a stick of furniture, but even if there had been it couldn't have given the rooms any style. The house was nothing but square, box-shaped cubicles, plastered walls and dingy red tile on the floor. The kitchen had one row of atrocious metal cabinets, a refrigerator that looked as though it had been born in the fifties and a stove to match.

The bathroom was more like a utility unit, as it also shared its space with a water heater and a clothes washer and dryer. The tub was an ancient one that stood on legs. It, and all the other fixtures, were stained a yellow mineral color. Maggie doubted they could ever be bleached white again.

She really wanted to weep and shout at the sight of it all, but found she was just too tired and overwhelmed to do either. And to add to her distress, there was no electricity or water. How stupid of her not to send her utility deposits ahead of time. She cursed herself for her neglect, even though she knew it would do no good.

So now what did she do? She was hot, exhausted and hungry. There was a little ice water left in her thermos for drinking, but not nearly enough to take a bath. She supposed she could eat some of the canned food Tony had insisted she take. Or she could drive back to Amarillo and rent a room until she could make this place accommodating, if that would ever be possible!

The thought of driving all the way back to Amarillo made up her mind for her. At least for tonight. She just didn't have the energy to make it that far. Besides, she had spent the past week in motels and hotels. She was sick of them and for some insane reason, she found she liked the silence surrounding this place. There was only the wind and the cranking of the old windmill to be heard. Astonishingly, she'd already gotten accustomed to the odd little creaks.

With sudden determination, she hurried through the house, opening every window in every room. The breeze outside smelled dusty, but fresh dust would be better than stale dust, she decided.

A few minutes later, she had carried in all her belongings from the Alfa Romeo. She had brought far too many clothes, but back in New York she had been indecisive as to how long she would stay in Texas, and to be honest, she still hadn't decided. However, that wasn't an immediate problem. Right now she was faced with no furniture and no power or water.

Maggie suddenly thought of the tank at the windmill. It was full of water. Was it clean enough to wash in? The question had her hurrying out the back door and across the barren ground. Cow hooves had once stomped the soft, damp ground around the tank, leaving deep holes that were now dry and hard caked, and Maggie stumbled awkwardly over them. When she swished her hands through the water, she found it to be a murky color, but it smelled clean and Maggie decided that once it grew dark, she would come back and take a bath.

The very thought of washing away all the sweat and dust from her body lifted her spirits immeasurably and she wanted to laugh that something that seemed so simple could make her so happy.

On closer inspection of the house, she discovered her uncle had apparently gotten rid of all his dishes, utensils and bed linens. She didn't understand it, especially if he had intended giving her the place all along, and it made her a little angry at George. She knew the anger was unjustified, especially since her uncle was dead, but she had driven almost two thousand miles to find a rundown house with nothing in it. Could it be that George had grown senile right before his death? Or maybe someone had stolen the things? But that didn't seem logical when both doors were securely locked and all the windows intact.

Oh, well, she decided, there was no use fretting about it now. Tonight she would sit down and make a list of all the things she needed. The cost didn't matter to Maggie. She had so much money now that she had lost count. No, money was no object, but it would be a nuisance to get all the things she needed from Amarillo out here, especially since her Alfa Romeo wouldn't carry very much. She would have to have everything shipped out here.

As these thoughts ran through her head, she realized that subconsciously she had already decided to stay. If she went to the trouble of getting the place furnished, she would at least have to stay a month to make the effort worthwhile.

What the house really needed was a complete remodeling. If she found the same sense of peace her uncle found here, then she might consider hiring a building contractor to work on the house. After all, it might be fun to redesign it herself.

The bath felt just as wonderful as Maggie had dreamed it would. As she poured the tepid water over her body, the soft breeze cooled her sunburned skin. Now that the glaring sun had slid down the flat horizon, it was much more bearable outside and Maggie took her time as she soaped her skin and long blond hair.

She had brought a flashlight along with her. Someone had warned her that Texas hosted rattlesnakes, so she thought it a wise move to watch her step beneath the beam of light.

She was thankful she had brought some beach towels. She wrapped one sarong-style around her, using another to dry her hair. As she made her way slowly back to the house, she absently fluffed the long strands out against the breeze to help the drying process. Her hair was well below her shoulder blades and permed into curly layers that floated around her face. She had worn it that way for a long time. André, her beauty consultant, kept it in beautiful condition, but sometimes she wished she could do what she wanted with it. However, that was out of the question. Phillip said her hair was her trademark, a style uniquely hers, and it would be disastrous to cut it or change it in any way.

Personally, Maggie didn't agree with him. She didn't think her career depended entirely on her hair, but Phillip was her agent and she was supposed to listen to his advice.

The sound of a car caught her attention. Fascinated because she had not noticed one since her arrival, she watched its progress along the gravel road.

Much to her dismay, it pulled in front of the house and parked beside her Alfa Romeo. On first impulse she wanted to run, but then she realized there wasn't anywhere *to* run. She was totally defenseless!

Her heart racing, she forced herself to calmly walk to the back of the house. Not that it could give her any protection if the person was out for mischief.

"There she is, Daddy," a little girl's voice said, floating out through the darkness.

Maggie lifted her flashlight and a second later, a man and a little girl holding on to his hand appeared at the side of the house. It was the pair she had seen at Tony's. Instead of easing her anxiety, the sight seemed to increase her unease all over again, for the pair looked nothing at all like the two she had seen this afternoon. Particularly the man. What had Tony called him? The initials R.J.?

She studied him beneath the dim light, her eyes furtively taking in the sharp crease of his gray summer slacks, the expensive cotton shirt tucked neatly in at his lean waist, the classic loafers on his feet. He was bareheaded, and even though his hair was windblown, she could see it had been cut professionally in a fashionable style.

The little girl was in a charming pink dress edged with Victorian lace, and her hair was pulled neatly into one long French braid. She was eyeing Maggie curiously, her little bow mouth tilted in a smile.

Maggie had never expected to see these two again in a million years, and the obvious change in their appearance left her completely astonished. Questions raced frantically in her mind, and she lowered the flashlight so that the circle of light bobbed on the dry weeds and grass beneath their feet. She hoped the man did not catch the dismay on her face.

"I suppose you're Maggie Winslow," he said as the two of them drew to a halt just a few steps away from Maggie.

She was surprised to hear him use her name, and she wondered if Tony had told him. "Yes," she answered without offering anything more. After all, he was a complete stranger, and she was hardly dressed for meeting people. In fact, it made her furious that he should be so immaculate while she was wearing a towel!

"I'm your neighbor, R.J. Buchanan. We live in the house just down the road. I was a friend of your uncle's." He looked down at the little girl by his side. "And this is Nugget, my daughter."

"How do you do," she said. This news was even more disturbing, and she wondered why they were here. Was there some reason pertaining to George that had brought them calling?

"Was there some message you needed to pass along?" she asked.

Even in the darkness she could see the smug lines etched on his craggy face. "We Texans like to make our neighbors feel welcome," he drawled.

From the tone of his voice, Maggie realized that he considered her rude. "Er—well, I would invite you in, but as I have no electricity and no water it would be rather useless, don't you agree?"

"You should have stopped by the power company when you came through Amarillo," he stated in a voice that said she must be utterly stupid for not thinking of it herself.

Maggie frowned. "Yes, perhaps I should have. But then I didn't know the power would be off."

She could feel his eyes on her, and she shifted restlessly. He did not look at her like other men did. Usually her beauty had men ogling or jumping to do her bidding. However, this man seemed to find her whole appearance rather distasteful.

"Dead people have no use for electricity," he replied rather callously, making Maggie draw in a sharp breath.

"Obviously," she retorted. "And they don't use furniture, dishes or linen. Could you possibly tell me what happened to it? Or is thievery usual out here?"

His lips curled into a cockeyed grin beneath the black mustache. "While your uncle was in the hospital, he heard of a family who lost their home to fire. He asked me to see that they got all of it. You see, George knew for a long time that he was dying. There was no need for him to keep anything."

Maggie listened to the growl of his Texas drawl, but her mind was suddenly struggling with the picture of her beloved George losing his health and finally his life.

"Did my uncle have all his senses up until he died?" It was a question she hated to ask, especially of this man. But it was something she just had to know.

"You mean, did he go off his rocker?" The child inaptly called Nugget blurted in surprise. "No, ma'am. Uncle George was smart, and nice, too," she added in childlike honesty.

R.J. chuckled as he spoke to Maggie. "I would say George had all his senses. He said there was no use leaving anything in the house for you, said you would want to change it all, anyway, because you had . . . class."

The last word came out mockingly, and Maggie bristled. This man didn't know her, but obviously he thought he did. Before she could think up a suitable retort, he was saying, "Of course, if you had shown enough compassion to have visited George once in a while, you would have known about his senses. It looks to me like a dying man in the hospital could have had at least one relative remember him."

How dared he judge her! It was true she hadn't visited her uncle, but it hadn't been all her fault.

"For your information, Mr. Buchanan, I'm a model," she started to explain, but his harshly spoken words stopped her.

"So? Is that some kind of affliction? Does that pardon you from personal responsibilities? Or does it simply mean a wad of money is where your heart should be?"

Never had she been spoken to this way, and the shock of it left her speechless. After a moment of tense silence, she shook the hair back over her shoulder with a haughty toss and said, "It would give me great pleasure if you would get off my property."

To her astonishment, he winked at her and then gave her a mocking little bow. "Ma'am, I'm sure my leaving will be as much a relief to me as it will to you," he said smoothly.

Maggie watched, her teeth gritting angrily, as the two of them turned and walked away.

As they neared their car, Maggie could hear Nugget saying in a perplexed voice, "But, Daddy, I thought you were going to ask her to stay?"

"Yes, Nugget," he answered tiredly. "I thought I was, too."

The words confused Maggie, but she quickly switched them out of her mind as their car pulled away and headed down the road. At the moment, all she wanted to think about was sleep and to forget she had ever seen a Mr. R.J. Buchanan.

She had brought an inflatable air mattress along for swimming, so she could use that for a bed. It took her a long time to blow it up, and she was dizzy by the time it was filled. Mr. R.J. Buchanan was so full of hot air that he could have probably blown it up with one breath, she thought nastily.

If she had shown any gumption at all where the man was concerned, she would have slapped his face. If it had been Phillip or any other man she would have. But there was an unexplainable toughness about R.J. Buchanan that had made her think twice about such retaliation. He was probably the sort of man who welcomed violence and would have thought nothing of slapping her back, probably even enjoying it, her mind tacked on.

Phillip had called this place uncivilized. That description might not have been far off the track if all the men turned out to be like her neighbor.

With angry movements, she smoothed a long chenille robe over the mattress so that she wouldn't have to lie next to the smothering vinyl. True, she had made a mistake about him. His expensive clothes had proved that much. But clothes did not a man make, and obviously R.J. Buchanan was a wolf in sheep's clothing.

Sitting on the edge of her newly made bed, Maggie picked up her compact and studied herself beneath the beam of the flashlight. God, she looked ghastly! Her skin was burned to a deep crimson and her eyes were bloodshot with tired dark circles beneath them. Heavens, what would her friends back in New York say if they could see her now? For one thing,

André would have a fit. The idea was very amusing, and for a moment Maggie chuckled at the image in the mirror.

Rummaging through her makeup kit, she pulled out a jar of skin cream and began to rub it into her face. It had been stupid of her to drive so far with the top down on her car. But waiting a day and a half to have a broken air conditioner repaired had quickly made her decide to just put the top down and be on her way.

Under usual circumstances, she could boast about her gorgeous skin, a necessity for a model. At times it was a nuisance to take care of, such as those times when she came home late at night, exhausted from a day of shooting. Yet she supposed the care she took with her appearance was worth it in the long run. After all, her face and body had made her a fortune. However, the way she looked right now, she doubted her looks could have earned her a penny.

She peered at the mirror a bit closer, wondering what R.J. Buchanan had been thinking of her looks. Had he thought her wide-set aquamarine eyes large and seductive? Her softly shaped lips the kind he wanted to kiss? Her firm breasts and long shapely legs the kind he liked to touch?

Maggie mentally slapped herself and put away the mirror. Apparently she had turned the man off, and she told herself that she definitely didn't care. Furthermore, she must be literally insane to be lusting after a married man with a child. Not to mention the fact that he was obviously an uncultivated boor.

She switched off the flashlight, rubbed more cream into her sore shoulders, then stretched out on the mattress, deliberately pushing the image of Mr. Buchanan from her mind.

Since it was Friday, her parents were probably at a party tonight. More than likely they were having cocktails right now, and later, boiled lobster, or maybe pheasant. They most definitely would not be eating beenie-weenies out of the open can with a plastic spoon as Maggie had done, nor would they be having a half-melted candy bar for dessert.

For a long time she thought about the contrast. Her parents had tried to persuade her to stay in New York, but their reasons had all seemed so businesslike and logical. Not at all emotional. But then her parents had never been emotional people. Neither of them would ever tell her that they didn't want her to go because they loved her and would worry about her.

Instead, Tomas Winslow had grunted, "You've a fortune here; there's nothing for you out there." And Rhoda, her mother, had wailed, "But what about my charity fashion show you promised for the literature club?"

Sighing, Maggie turned onto her stomach, the memory of her uncle suddenly invading her thoughts. George had been an emotional, affectionate man. She supposed that was why she had loved him so. It grated on her to think R.J. Buchanan thought she hadn't cared, because she really had. The truth of it was that she had not found out about his illness with diabetes until the news of his death had caught up to her in Puerto Rico where she and two other models had been doing a layout of swimwear for a famous sports magazine.

The news had hit her hard and she'd wanted to fly back and attend the funeral. But that would have delayed the shooting and ruined the budget. Not that she couldn't have thwarted the advertising agency. She was in such demand that she could afford to do anything and get away with it. However, Phillip had reasoned that attending George's funeral would not help her uncle, so she had stayed, inwardly grieving while putting on a facade for the camera.

Still, lingering in the back of her consciousness was the knowledge that she could have visited George on other occasions. Maybe R.J. Buchanan had been right. Had she been thinking of money and her career to such an extent that she had become heartless?

She hated the man for throwing such a seed of doubt into her mind. Yet it was there, anyway. And no matter who had put it there, it was a question that needed to be faced.

Thinking back, she had to admit that when her career had taken off, she'd been riding on a cloud and for a while she had lived fast. Very fast. George had not entered her mind too much then. She had been too busy being a famous beauty, hitting the glamor spots and partying with the supposedly "in" crowd.

But Maggie hadn't been foolish enough to let that kind of life lead her down the wrong path. Yet there had been a time in her life when she had been very foolish. Men seemed to have a knack for making women act like idiots. And that was what she had been upon meeting Mario; suave, sophisticated, Mario. Who for a while had swept Maggie off her feet with his zest for living. He was good-looking, charming and very successful as a fashion photographer. He was also a fraud. That could be the only way to sum him up. Maggie had discovered the hard way that behind that smooth facade there was a selfish child who used people and then laughed about it.

For weeks he had tried to get her into bed with him, but Maggie had held back, some inner voice warning her to be cautious even though Mario seemed like the dream man she had been searching for. In the end it was just as well that she had held back.

One night in New York they had had a terrible quarrel about it, and Maggie had left his hotel room in a black rage. A few hours later, she decided to go back and try to work things out between them. It was then she'd discovered Mario in bed with someone else and the look on his face when she had entered the room said, Too bad, you had your chance.

Yes, that had been the time she'd needed her other daddy, George, but she had been too ashamed to face him or tell him what had happened. Now she wished above all else that she had. He would have helped her to realize that her life wasn't over just because she had thought herself in love with a useless playboy.

Maggie smiled in the darkness, glad that she could now think of Mario without any pain or longing, or any kind of feeling at all. She smiled, too, because never again would she be susceptible to any man's charm.

Chapter Three

A knock on the door woke her the next morning. Startled out of her sleep, Maggie wrapped the white chenille robe around her and padded to the door barefoot.

Much to her amazement, she found R.J. and Nugget on the front step. The little girl was holding a thermos bottle, and in R.J.'s hands was a tray covered with aluminum foil and resting on top was a wildflower similar to the black-eyed Susan. Mouth-watering smells of cooked food were wafting from the tray and Maggie's empty stomach grumbled at the temptation.

"Good morning, Maggie," the little girl said with a grin. "We brought you some breakfast 'cause we knew you couldn't turn the stove on."

Maggie was stunned. She had never expected to see either of them again after the words they had exchanged last night. She looked from Nugget to R.J. for some kind of explanation.

The man's gold-brown eyes looked straight into Maggie's. "Last night—well, George was a good friend of mine," R.J. said a bit ruefully. "No, he was more than that. For eight years he was like a brother. His death—" He took off his cap, then settled it back on the dark brown curls in a movement of agitation. "I guess I found it too easy to take it out on you."

Maggie swallowed to ease the ache in her throat. The memory of dear George, coupled with the fact that this strange man didn't despise her, pulled at the softer side of her emotions. She didn't know why. Especially after last night when she had assured herself that she abhorred the man.

"Regrets aren't very easy to live with, Mr. Buchanan, and I'll always regret not seeing my uncle before he died," she responded.

He nodded in understanding and extended the tray. There wasn't any way that she could refuse without appearing to be a snob, and for some reason unknown to her she wanted to prove to this man and his daughter that she wasn't one.

"Thank you," she said, reaching for the laden tray. "I'm sure I'll enjoy it. Would you like to come in?"

"I've got to go back to the house and feed the horses, but if you'd like, I could light the pilots on your stove and water heater," R.J. offered.

Maggie gazed at him, wondering if the offer was sincerely given. It was hard to tell from his expression.

"That would be nice of you," she murmured, pulling open the screen door to allow R.J. and Nugget to precede her into the house.

"I haven't paid my deposit at the gas company, either, so there probably isn't any gas," she speculated, sitting down on the air mattress to partake of the breakfast food.

He waved away her words and started toward the kitchen. Maggie noticed he was dressed similarly to the way he was yesterday—a pair of Levi's and brown, heavily scuffed cowboy boots and a white polo shirt. What intrigued her the most was the company emblem on his cap. Buchanan Construction Co. Perhaps his father was a builder, she thought.

"You don't need to go to the gas company. You have your own propane tank in the backyard," he called back to her. "All you have to do is turn it on at the tank."

Maggie began to roll back the foil on the tray as she listened to this information. "But where does the gas come from?"

"Whenever your tank gets low, you call a propane company in Amarillo and they bring it out in a big truck and pump it into your tank," he explained.

"Then of course I would appreciate your turning it on for me."

His answer was the slam of the back door, and Maggie supposed he had gone out to the tank.

Nugget settled herself on the air mattress close to Maggie, a grin on her gamine face.

The food was delicious and plentiful. There were scrambled eggs, several slices of buttered toast, crisp bacon, tomato juice, coffee and a little container of honey for the toast.

Maggie dug in unashamedly, for she was starved after her meager meal the previous night. Back home, she usually just ate yogurt or a vitamin-filled drink for breakfast. She had to admit this was a pleasant change, even if it did add a pound to her figure.

"Did your mother cook all this?" Maggie asked after she had taken several bites. "It's very delicious."

Nugget's brown eyes widened. "Oh, no," she said very seriously. "My real mother and daddy died when I was a baby. R.J. is my daddy now." Then she grinned and wiggled upon the mattress. "He does all the cooking, but he's teaching me how, and I'm learning real fast, he says."

Maggie smiled gently, even though she was inwardly shocked. "I'm sure you are," she said, reaching thoughtfully for her coffee cup.

So this wasn't R.J.'s child from birth, and from the sound of it, he wasn't married. It puzzled her because the child obviously favored him. Still, for some ridiculous reason, the news that R.J. wasn't married seemed to brighten the whole place.

"Shouldn't you be going to school? I'll bet you're eight years old, aren't you?"

Nugget nodded. "I was eight in April. But I don't need to go to school. We're already out for the summer."

"Oh, that's nice. I'm sure you'll have fun on vacation."

The girl's little bow-shaped mouth suddenly drooped. "I would if I didn't have to go to work with Daddy. He's afraid to let me stay home by myself. He says I might get cut or snakebit and then no one would know."

"I believe your daddy is right," Maggie stressed as she crunched into the toast. "Sometimes accidents happen."

"I guess," the girl admitted reluctantly, tugging one of her long blond braids. "But it's boring at the office. If we went out to the sites all the time, then it would be fun."

Maggie wondered what kind of office and what kind of sites the girl was talking about, but didn't ask the question. She wasn't going to be guilty of pumping an innocent child for information.

"Your hair is very pretty," Maggie remarked. "I could never have braided mine like that when I was your age."

Nugget glowed at the compliment, and Maggie noticed the freckles scattered across her tip-tilted nose brightened her brown eyes even more. "Oh, I can't do it yet, either, but I'm learning. I can put it in a ponytail all by myself, but Daddy braids it for me. When we go somewhere dressed up, he French-braids it for me, too."

"How nice," Maggie murmured. She couldn't picture such a tough looking guy doing anything of the sort, but he must have done, since obviously there was only him and this engaging child. "Tell me," Maggie went on, "is your real name Nugget?"

Nugget giggled. "That's my nickname. Daddy gave it to me when I was a baby and came to live with him. Emmaline is my real name. He says that will be nice when I grow to be a woman. But right now it's a little bit too big for me."

Maggie smiled and nodded, and Nugget continued in childlike animation. "Do you know why he calls me Nugget?"

"No, why?" Maggie went along with the question.

"Because he says I'm worth more than a big gold nugget to him."

"That's very sweet," Maggie admitted. Obviously this child was devoted to her adoptive father and he to her.

Footsteps had Maggie looking up from her plate to see R.J. standing in the doorway to the kitchen. "The gas is on, and there don't seem to be any leaks outside. If you happen to have some matches, I'll get the stove going for you."

Maggie shook her head. "I do have a cigarette lighter."

"That will probably work."

Maggie set the food aside and searched through her purse. When she found the elegant gold lighter, she walked over and handed it to R.J. He started toward the stove and Maggie followed, anxious to see if the antique would really work.

R.J. removed the top of the burners, then started to flip open the lighter, but before he did, he glanced down at the real gold case with the row of diamonds along one side and read the inscription—Love, Mario. His thick brown brows lifted coyly before he sparked it to a flame and Maggie found herself wanting to say there was no Mario in her life, that she only had the lighter because it was too expensive to throw away. She wanted to say these things but she didn't. It would sound utterly ridiculous. This man didn't need or want an explanation from her, and she shouldn't feel obliged to give him one.

After fetching a screwdriver from his jeep, R.J. adjusted the burners on the stove, turned them off, tried them again, then started toward the bathroom to deal with the water heater.

Maggie followed, watching his easy stride as they walked down the narrow hallway.

"Perhaps you could tell me where I find the public works authority to have the water turned on?" she asked.

"Ma'am, you don't have city water out here. All you need to do is turn on the electricity and you'll have water."

"I beg your pardon?"

He halted at the bathroom door, and Maggie nearly collided with him as he turned to answer.

She reached out and touched the wall to regain her balance, and as she did, she noticed that he was perhaps only an inch or two above her five foot eight. It was a disturbing discovery, because he was standing only a short space away from her and as she looked into his strong face, she realized it would be so easy to kiss him. Their lips would be on the same level—their bodies matched so perfectly.

"You have well water," his voice interrupted her fantasies. "An electric motor pumps it into the house. If you'll give me a call after work tonight, I'll prime it and get it running for you."

"That's very generous of you," she said, trying to shake off the mental picture she had of the two of them. What kind of effect was this place having on her? She had never had this problem around a man before. And to make her feel even more shameless, she had to admit that this man had never looked at her in any kind of suggestive way.

R.J. shrugged, one corner of his mustache lifting into a grin. His smile focused Maggie's eyes on his mouth, and she noticed again how white his teeth were next to his deeply tanned skin. For the first time, she wondered about his age and guessed that it couldn't be more than thirty-three.

"It's the least I can do for George's niece."

He lit the hot water heater and assured Maggie there was enough water in it to keep it from exploding before she got the water working properly.

"Let's go, Nugget," he announced, once they were back in the living room.

The girl jumped up from the air mattress and grabbed R.J. by the hand. "Oh, can't I stay until you feed the horses, Daddy? I want to talk with Maggie some more."

"You haven't been invited, and Maggie may have things to do," R.J. reminded the child.

"Of course she can stay," Maggie spoke up, seeing the little girl's disappointed expression. Being an only child, Maggie rarely had the opportunity to be around children. She didn't know much about their habits, but this one seemed to be well mannered and she couldn't do anything right at the moment, anyway. "I'm sure I'll enjoy her company."

Nugget danced at the invitation and R.J. said, "Well, okay, babe. But I'll pick you up in thirty minutes, so don't give me any delay tactics then."

The child nodded and blew him a kiss as he walked out the front door.

After he had started the jeep and driven away, Maggie went back to her breakfast, taking immense pleasure in pouring herself another cup of coffee from the thermos.

"You're a model, aren't you?" Nugget asked as she walked around the bare living room.

"Yes, I am."

Nugget sighed dreamily. "I'll bet it must be fun."

"Sometimes," Maggie agreed. "But sometimes it's awfully hard work."

"That's what Uncle George said. He said you worked too hard and that you made piles and piles of money."

Maggie's eyes lifted from the plate to look at Nugget. Had George really summed up her life in that way? "Did you know my Uncle George very well?"

The child nodded briefly, then suddenly her face grew sad. "I cried for a long time when he died. But R.J. said now that George was in heaven, he wasn't sick anymore, so that makes it better. It was awful to see him sick. Daddy went to see him every day in the hospital. He took him good things to eat, like hamburgers. But I had to wait down in the lobby because I was too young to go in the room."

Maggie swallowed to ease the ache in her throat. "I'm sure George knew you were sitting down there thinking about him."

"Oh, sure. I drew him lots of pictures and wrote lots of letters so Daddy could take them up to him."

And I sent him nothing, Maggie thought desolately. I never called, never showed my face while he was leaving this world. It was a sad thought to know that this child had been closer to her own uncle than she had been.

"I'll bet Texas isn't anything like New York. But Texas is nice, don't you think?"

Maggie smiled hesitantly, wondering what this child or anyone could find pleasant about this dusty, windblown place. "Well, it's certainly different. I imagine I'll like it much better once I get my house fixed."

Nugget nodded and skipped over to the air mattress. "You do need something to sit on and sleep on."

"Perhaps I'll go into Amarillo today and buy some furniture. Maybe your daddy would let you go with me?" she suggested, on second thought. "You could show me the way around the city."

Nugget's brown eyes widened with excitement. "Would you ask him, Maggie? I'll bet he would say yes if you asked him."

"Of course I'll ask him. Surely he won't care if you go," Maggie said, pushing herself up from the makeshift bed.

She began to look around the main living area, wondering how she could possibly improve it. Drapes, wall hangings, perhaps a huge braided rug? It seemed hopeless. "I really wish I could have the house remodeled. It is rather run-down," she told Nugget as the little girl followed in her footsteps. "Don't you think it needs help?"

"Well, it doesn't look too good," Nugget admitted. "I think it needs Daddy to work on it. He could make it really pretty."

Maggie glanced down at the girl's face. "What do you mean?"

"Daddy is a carpenter. He's an engineer, too," Nugget proudly announced. "He owns the Buchanan Construction Company."

Maggie's winged brows lifted at this bit of information. "You mean he builds things?"

Nugged nodded. "Houses and office buildings. Things like that. And they always look pretty, so I know he could make this house pretty, too."

"Maybe he could, at that," Maggie replied absently, the wheels of her mind already spinning rapidly. She hadn't expected building to be the man's profession. She had expected him to be something like a dump-truck driver or auto mechanic. However, now that she actually knew what he did for a living, she wondered if he would consider doing this house. For some reason, she knew he would be excellent at the job. There was something about him that assured Maggie he would be. And with him living right down the road, and she here, it would make things much easier than if she were back in New York.

She looked up at Nugget questioningly. "Do you think he would consider doing it?"

"Sure," she said knowingly.

Nugget kept up a stream of chatter until R.J. pulled back in front of the house. He left the motor running and honked for Nugget. Maggie followed the child outside. She didn't feel self-conscious about this man seeing her in the robe she still wore. After all, the second time she'd seen him, she'd been wearing a towel.

As Nugget climbed into the jeep, R.J. said, "Did you need something else, Maggie?"

That damned voice of his, Maggie thought. In plays and movies she had heard accents that were supposed to have been Texan. But now she knew the exaggerated hillbilly twang had been way off base. This man's voice was very distinct—very seductive.

"As a matter of fact, there is. If you have a minute," she added.

He switched off the motor and turned to give her his full attention. It was a disarming move on his part, to say the least.

"Nugget was telling me you're a builder," she said.

"That's right." He grinned. "But if she told you I build skyscrapers, you shouldn't have believed her."

While he'd been gone Maggie had wrapped her hair into a soft knot on top of her head and impulsively stuck the little flower he and Nugget had given her into the base of it. She saw his eyes find it and felt her cheeks go pink.

Maggie laughed softly. "Well, I wasn't really wanting a skyscraper. Just a little remodeling done in the house."

His brows lifted with interest, and Maggie noticed what a strong, straight nose he had, and how shiny his dark hair was. "How much remodeling?"

She shrugged noncommittally. "I don't really know. Perhaps you would have some good ideas about that. But I was thinking of knocking out partitions and doing something with the walls and floors. I'm not really fond of plaster and tile."

He chuckled and then studied her thoughtfully, as if he had his own ideas about her proposition. Maggie's eyes went to his body. It was difficult not to when his tight clothing showed off every hard line. His chest was wide, the thick pectoral muscles well defined, and she wondered what it would be like to lay her cheek against it, to take off his cap and let that shiny dark hair slide through her fingers.

"I'll tell you what," he said finally, breaking into Maggie's rather carnal thoughts. "I'll take the job, but on one condition."

"What is it?" Maggie asked a little warily. "If it's paying you in advance, that's no problem. I can have whatever you need wired today."

His mouth curved into a mocking line. "That's the condition. I don't want to be paid with money."

Maggie's breath sucked in harshly. How could he be so crass? And right here in front of his own daughter!

"Oh?" she said tartly. "How would you like to be paid, Mr. Buchanan?"

R.J. chuckled and shook his head wondrously at her sudden offense. "Ma'am, this isn't New York. You've got it all wrong. I need a housekeeper. Someone to look after Nugget."

Maggie's cheeks blazed with deep color. What could he possibly be thinking of her assumption? And why did this man unknowingly steer her thoughts into such sexual directions?

"Oh, I see," she managed to get out. For some reason this condition was even a greater shock than the one she had first believed him to want.

"I'm glad you do." He grinned, and for the first time since she had met him, there was something of a sensual glint in his eyes. Perhaps the man was normal, after all!

Maggie cleared her throat and looked down at Nugget, who was following their conversation with rapt attention. "Then I'm afraid you had better forget the job, because I know very little about cooking or housekeeping, or children, either."

He shrugged as if her admission made no difference. "Neither have the other women I've tried so far, so I'm willing to take the chance. Aren't you, Nugget?"

"I sure am," the child breathed excitedly.

"But...but I didn't really come out here to work," Maggie stuttered.

"What had you planned on doing?" R.J. asked.

The question befuddled her. What had she planned on doing? Nothing? Had it been the way Phillip had said—she was coming out here to escape? No, she wasn't wanting to escape. She was wanting to search and find and live a life, if only for a while, outside the one she had known. Well, here's your chance, Maggie she silently told herself. But on the other hand, to take on a job of this sort would be so demanding. Furthermore, even though they had known George quite well, she hardly knew these people.

"If it makes any difference, I'd rather you live at my house. That way your house will be empty and much easier to work in, plus the fact that you won't have to eat and sleep through sawdust and hammering," R.J. added persuasively.

It sounded logical, even inviting, to Maggie. She could have the house fixed as she wanted, then pick out some nice furniture after the work was completed. But on the other hand, she didn't know if it would be wise to be that close to R.J. Buchanan. She was already having fantasies about him. What would living in the same house bring on? She looked at Nugget, and the girl's eyes were glowing with excited anticipation. The sight of her made up Maggie's mind. After all, she contemplated, what could happen with an eight-year-old for a chaperone? Besides the fact that Mr. Buchanan seemed totally indifferent to her.

"Well, what do you say, Maggie? Or do you have commitments back in the Big Apple?"

Maggie shook her head with sudden conviction. "No, I plan to stay all summer." Just when this decision had been reached, she didn't know, but the words seemed to be tumbling out of her on their own will. "So I'll take the offer."

"That's great, isn't it, Nugget?" R.J. asked the girl.

"I'll say," she breathed excitedly, then looked at her dad with earnestness. "Can I stay home with Maggie every day?"

"You may," he answered with an indulgent grin.

"Will you take me and her to Palo Duro or maybe even to Albuquerque?"

"If Maggie would like to."

"And can she go with us to your ball games and when we go into Amarillo to shop and eat ice cream?"

"If she wants to go."

Nugget looked up at Maggie with an endearing smile "You will want to, won't you, Maggie? It's super fun."

They didn't sound like outings suited for a housekeeper yet Maggie couldn't help but smile back. "If you say it' fun, then I wouldn't possibly want to miss it."

R.J. extended his hand to Maggie, and unexpectedly he heart lurched as she placed hers into it. "I guess this mean we have a deal, then, Maggie."

Maggie nodded, wondering why his rough palm should excite her so. "Yes, I guess we do."

R.J. looked at his daughter. "Okay, Nugget, you can stay and help Maggie take her things to the house and show he where everything is." His tawny eyes flickered over to Maggie. "My number is by the phone if you need me for any thing. Otherwise, I'll be home at six."

She nodded and said, "Would it be all right for Nugge and me to go into the city later today and see about th electricity?" She didn't want to bother about having it re connected just yet if it wasn't necessary.

"Of course it will be fine," he assured her.

Another thought struck her, and she asked, "Er, hov long should I plan on being your housekeeper?"

He studied her for a moment, then shrugged. "That' hard to say, Maggie. We have four houses and two rathe large office buildings going right now, so I'm afraid I'll have to work on yours at night. It could take most of the sum mer.'' The lines in his cheeks deepened, and he asked rather tauntingly, ''Want to back out, now that you know how involved it will be?''

She hesitated, but only for a second. Her mind was made up. Right or wrong, she was going to venture into this thing. ''No,'' she said with a shake of her head.

He smiled, making Maggie's breath catch in her throat at his attractiveness. However, she didn't have long to ponder his looks because he quickly started the jeep and pulled it into gear.

''If everything is settled, I'll see you two girls tonight,'' he said as the jeep began to roll away from Nugget and Maggie.

''Bye, Daddy. I'll be good,'' Nugget sang out.

Maggie watched him drive away, the dust swirling around the back of the jeep.

Of all the men she had met in her lifetime, why did she have the desire to know this one better? They were from opposite ends of the earth. He would no more fit into her life-style than she into his. Just remember that Maggie, she rudely reminded herself.

A pair of thin little arms wrapped tightly around her waist brought Maggie back to the present and she looked bemusedly down at Nugget. The child's face was as happy as if it were Christmas.

''This is going to be the best summer ever,'' Nugget said, beaming.

''Maybe you're right,'' Maggie replied, wishing she still had the faith of a child.

Chapter Four

A housekeeper! A baby-sitter! Maggie's head swam with the implications of the words. What had caused her to agree to take on such a task? And furthermore, what had prompted R. J. Buchanan to offer it to her in the first place? She must have had a temporary lapse of sanity. What other reason could there be for such a rash decision?

These questions rattled around in Maggie's head as she and Nugget began to pack her things into the Alfa Romeo. The more she thought about it, the more she concluded that Mr. R. J. Buchanan either possessed an enormous amount of nerve or he was very good at hiding his true motives. Obviously he knew she was a famous model. George was bound to have talked about her career at one time or another. So had R.J. merely offered her the job as a degrading slap in the face? Did he want to have her working for him as a hired hand merely so he could brag to his friends that he had the famous model Maggie Winslow as his live-in maid?

Somehow Maggie doubted that. He didn't seem the sort of man who would need or want to brag about anything. This is ridiculous, she thought suddenly, pulling herself to a mental halt. Why was she wondering if R. J. Buchanan had ulterior motives? The man had seen a situation where both of them could benefit, and that was the sum of it.

An hour later, Maggie found out for herself just how badly R. J. Buchanan needed a housekeeper. On first glance, the house seemed to be in shambles, being littered with dirty dishes, which were not confined entirely to the kitchen, dirty clothes, newspapers and magazines, toys, tools, crushed beer cans and shoes. The list of items increased as Nugget took her on a tour of the house. The beds were unmade and looked as though that was their permanent condition.

Maggie shook her head as she brushed a wisp of hair back from her forehead. "Nugget," she asked in an awed tone, "does the house always look this way?"

Nugget's little face became thoughtful. "Well, most of the time. But sometimes me and Daddy get it all cleaned up spick-and-span. Then sometimes Daddy just wants to rest after he gets home from work. And I haven't learned how to do all the housecleaning yet."

Maggie shook her head at Nugget's apologetic expression. "I'm sure you do what you can. But what happened to your other housekeepers?"

Nugget shrugged with childlike candor. "Well, the first one was old and she thought me and R.J. were too messy. One got tired of driving all the way from the city out here. Then there was one who was young and pretty. She was all right until she started making goo-goo eyes at Daddy, so he kicked her out."

Maggie digested this information with a bit of dismay. "What happened after that?" she asked rather warily, almost afraid to hear the answer.

Nugget did a seemingly necessary pirouette before replying, "After that, he stopped hiring housekeepers. He said he liked it better with just me and him, anyway."

So where did that leave her? Maggie wondered. Just a tolerated necessity? It would be a long summer if that was the case.

"But I know R.J. will like having you here, 'cause he likes pretty girls," Nugget continued, trying to reassure Maggie.

As long as they didn't make goo-goo eyes at him, Maggie silently tacked on. "Oh, does your daddy have many girlfriends?" She knew it wasn't right to be asking this of the child, but her curiosity about the man increased with each passing moment.

Nugget frowned disgustedly, then skipped over to the laden kitchen cabinet to pull a half-eaten caramel sucker from a piece of wax paper. She licked it enthusiastically, then said, "Daddy dates a lot. Sometimes I get to meet them, sometimes I don't. When he goes out with one of them, I stay with Helen, and that's fun, 'cause she's nice."

Maggie decided she had stood still long enough and moved toward the sink. "Who is Helen?" she asked as she squirted liquid soap beneath the stream of hot water.

"Helen is a friend that lives down the road," the little girl supplied easily. "Do you know what she calls Daddy?"

Maggie turned to look over her shoulder at Nugget. The child had laid down her sucker and was now gathering the dirty silverware from the table.

"No, what does she call him?" Maggie responded, knowing even as she asked that it wasn't right for her to continue a conversation of this sort. She should be discouraging Nugget from talking about her father, but that would hardly be possible when he seemed to be the center of the child's world. Or at least that excuse relieved Maggie's conscience.

Nugget brought the silverware over to the cabinet and placed it within Maggie's reach. "She says Daddy is a moonlight bandit. Isn't that a funny thing to call a man?"

"I've never heard that phrase before," Maggie had to admit.

"She says it's because R.J. is such a charmer that he steals all the ladies' hearts. Do you think he'll steal yours, Maggie?" Nugget asked with the frank innocence of a child.

For a moment Maggie imagined herself in the silver moonlight, R.J.'s strong profile close to hers, his lips murmuring something forbidden before they closed over her own parted ones. The image evoked a strange sort of shiver through her body, and she quickly shook her head and laughed in an effort to vanquish it. "No, Nugget. I'm a girl who keeps a hand on her heart at all times, so that way no man can steal it, even your daddy."

Nugget giggled. "I'll bet Daddy could steal it, anyway, 'cause he's so handsome. Don't you think so, Maggie?"

Maggie sighed as she dipped several plates into the soapy water. She hoped the question was not an example of exchanges she and Nugget would have all summer.

"Well, yes, I guess your daddy is handsome," she reluctantly agreed, telling herself as she said it that it was only to keep from hurting this sweet child's feelings. "But I know lots of handsome men back in New York."

"Oh."

From Nugget's crestfallen expression, Maggie saw it was obvious she didn't want to believe any man could compare to her daddy.

"Come on," Maggie urged with a smile. "Help me clean the kitchen and then I'll show you some of my things when I unpack them. How would that be?"

Nugget was suddenly all smiles again. "Oh, that'll be super!" she exclaimed and skipped back to the table for more dishes.

On a second look, Maggie realized the house was very nice. Apparently R.J. had used his skills as a carpenter to improve the interior, and his efforts showed in the rich wood on the walls and the intricately carved cornice boards over the windows and also in the kitchen with its walls of beautiful ash cabinets. The furniture, floors and drapes were in Mexican style. Rich browns, soft cream with splashes of bright orange and yellow were both serviceable and pleasing to the eye. The effect was everything she had expected in George's house but hadn't found.

By the time they had straightened the living room and Nugget's bedroom, Maggie's knot of hair had fallen to her shoulders, where it clung uncomfortably to the sweaty skin of her neck and shoulders. Her makeup felt as if it had turned to mud on her face, and she had broken one of her nails while changing the sheets on Nugget's bed.

"It's lunchtime," Maggie said wearily as she smoothed the last wrinkle from the pink bedspread. "Let's have something to eat and then we'll drive to Amarillo. There's no way we can clean the whole house today!"

Nugget followed her down the hallway to the kitchen. "What about the laundry, Maggie? When are we going to do it?"

Stunned, Maggie turned in her tracks to stare at the child. "The laundry! Where is it?" she asked. She hoped R.J. kept it better than the house.

Nugget led her through a door of the kitchen and into a small utility room. There were a new washer and dryer, but piles of dirty clothes were heaped on the floor. And she hadn't even picked up the clothes strewn in R.J.'s room yet! What had she gotten herself into? Was this going to be worth improving a house that more than likely she would only visit occasionally? She must have been literally mad to take this on!

"Do you know how to work these things?" Maggie asked with exasperation.

Nugget nodded, her brown eyes wide in disbelief. "Gee, don't you?"

Maggie shook her head. Trying to come to a logical conclusion, Nugget said, "Oh, I'll bet you don't wash your clothes. You probably buy new ones when they get dirty."

"No, Nugget. I send them out to the cleaners and they bring them back all clean and ready to wear. I . . . I don't know how to do laundry!" she admitted on a tired wail.

The little girl seemed unperturbed by this bit of news. "That's no big deal. I'll show you. I've helped Daddy lots of times."

Nugget proceeded to show her how to sort the clothes, then fill and load the washer. It didn't appear quite as complicated as Maggie had first thought, but still she breathed a sigh of relief when the washer finally clicked off and she could see for herself that the clothes were all still intact.

After Nugget's favorite lunchtime fare, bologna sandwiches and grape Kool-aid, Maggie sent the child off to the bathroom to wash before their drive into the city.

Maggie supposed she should change clothes for the trip, but it seemed rather useless when she had more work waiting for her when she returned—especially if R.J. expected her to have some kind of meal prepared for tonight. Since she was an unreliable cook, she expected the task to take several hours, so she needed every minute she could spare.

Quickly she tied her hair into a ponytail with a purple ribbon to match her shorts and top. Instead of removing and reapplying her makeup, she dabbed on a bit of face powder, then added a touch of wine-colored lip gloss. She hardly expected anyone in Amarillo to recognize her. And if they did, it didn't matter. Out here she was going to be Maggie Winslow the person, not the model.

"I love your car, Maggie," Nugget exclaimed, wiggling excitedly in the seat. "It's almost as pretty as Daddy's."

Maggie slid her eyes off the road momentarily to look over at the girl. "What kind of car does your daddy have? I didn't see one parked at the house."

They were traveling slowly down the gravel road, and the hot afternoon sun was beating down on them. Obviously Nugget was accustomed to the fierce heat of the sun. Her skin was tanned a deep brown and was as smooth as honey—a far cry from Maggie's sore, burned skin.

"He keeps it parked in the garage. It's a Mustang convertible. Daddy says it's a classic. It was made in 1964—that was way before I was born."

"Yes, I'm certain of that." Maggie smiled indulgently as she adjusted the sunglasses on her nose. She was surprised to hear of the car. One of those cowboy pickup trucks was more of the type of vehicle she had expected a man like R.J. to drive. But then, how would she know? She was from New York, a world away from this sun-scorched land.

"We have a 1957 Chevrolet, too. It's red, and the inside is white. It's super! Daddy bought it as a pile of junk, then he worked on it at nights and then he had a man fix the engine. It's a classic, too. Did you know that, Maggie?"

Maggie nodded, surprised even further by Nugget's disclosures. Obviously the man was multitalented. "So which one do you prefer? The Mustang or the Chevy?"

Nugget's expressive little face became thoughtful, then after a moment, she broke into a wide grin. "The Mustang, 'cause Daddy puts down the top and takes me cruisin'. And that's fun!"

Maggie's brows lifted to an incredulous arch. "Cruisin'?"

"Yeah, you know—cruise around the city streets. Daddy always gets us a Coke or milkshake. He says that when I get to be a teenager, cruisin' will be one of my favorite things to do."

"Perhaps it will," Maggie replied, but without much conviction. She couldn't really say. She had never done most of the things that normal teenagers do. She had spent her early years training to be a model. Funny that this child and her father should remind her of the loss.

After Maggie found the power company, it was only a few minutes until she had deposited the money and she and Nugget were on their way again.

"Can you direct me to a shopping center, Nugget? I need to get some medicine for my sunburn."

"Sure," Nugget said agreeably. "I'll show you where me and Daddy buy our groceries and sometimes he lets me get a toy."

With Nugget's help, the cluster of shops was easy to locate. As they walked across the wide expanse of parking area, several people departed through the building's big double doors. Maggie paid them little notice, yet as she and Nugget drew closer, a young, extremely attractive woman halted a few steps away from them.

"Emmaline, is that you?" the woman asked as her eyes narrowed curiously on Maggie.

Maggie stared back, seeing a smoothly made-up face, dark shoulder-length hair and deep hazel eyes with an exotic slant to them. The woman was dressed very fashionably in a dress of white poplin that did nice things for her curvaceous figure. For perhaps the first time in her life, Maggie felt at a disadvantage.

Nugget edged closer to Maggie, clutching her hand as if seeking protection from this chic brunette. "Yes, Miss Woods," Nugget said solemnly.

"What are you doing in the city? Isn't R.J. with you?" the woman questioned in her cool Texas drawl.

Nugget shook her head and grinned conspiratorially up at Maggie. "Daddy's at work. Me and Maggie came to town together. Maggie's going to live with us all summer long," Nugget proudly announced.

The woman's dark pencil-thin brows lifted into a shocked arc, then suddenly she smiled reassuringly at Maggie. "I suppose you must be a relative," she said. "I know R.J. has many of them in Corpus Christi."

Maggie could not keep the faint smile from her lips. "I wouldn't know about that, Miss Woods, because I'm not a relative. Actually, I only arrived from New York just yesterday."

The words brought a scandalous expression to the woman's hazel eyes and painted red lips. "Er, I didn't catch your name."

Maggie's lips curved into a wry smile. "It's Maggie Winslow," she supplied, wondering why she was taking the time to even talk to this nosy female. As far as Maggie was concerned, if this woman wanted explanations she could go to R.J.

"Maggie's a famous model," Nugget piped up. "She's got stacks of money and lots of diamond rings!"

The woman's nostrils flared disdainfully at Nugget's announcement, and Maggie nudged the child while giving her a reproachful look. "Miss Woods is not interested in that, Nugget." She glanced back at the brunette with a definite purpose. "If you'll excuse us, our time is limited."

The woman was suddenly frosty at being given the brush-off, and her eyes gleamed with speculation as she studied Maggie and the child still clinging to her hand. "Certainly. Maybe we'll meet again soon. In fact, I'm sure we will."

Maggie wondered if that was a threat or a promise, as the woman departed with a click of high heels. Either way, if she never saw the woman again, it would be too soon for her. Something about Miss Woods had put her instantly on the defensive, and she told herself it was definitely not because she was one of R.J.'s girlfriends. She wouldn't have liked her under any circumstances.

"That was one of Daddy's girlfriends," Nugget supplied unnecessarily as the two of them made their way into the huge department store.

"Yes, I thought as much," Maggie absently replied as she tried to imagine R.J. with the supercilious Miss Woods. It was a difficult task, for they seemed direct opposites.

"Her name is Darla. Isn't that just too mushy?" Nugget mimicked.

Maggie tried to hide the smile she was feeling. "Nugget, you shouldn't talk about people," she admonished lightly. She couldn't bring herself to be any sterner with the child. Not when she was actually thinking the same thing.

By now they were on the cosmetic's aisle, and Nugget shuffled her feet as Maggie searched for the type of cream she wanted.

"I can't help it," the little girl said in a petulant voice. "She always wants Daddy all to herself. She doesn't like children. Especially me. And she thinks she's sooo pretty. But I don't. When we were at Tony's yesterday, I told Daddy I thought you were the prettiest woman ever."

Maggie smiled warmly at the child. For some reason the compliment from this girl meant much more than the ones she had received in the past. Maybe it was because she had felt so disheveled compared to Miss Woods's fashionable dress and dark beauty.

"Thank you, Nugget. That's very sweet of you."

The girl suddenly giggled, and her face turned pink as she clamped her hand over her mouth.

"What's wrong?" Maggie laughed. "Didn't you really mean it?"

Grinning broadly, Nugget said, "Yes, but you'd be angry if you knew what Daddy said."

Maggie's brows lifted as she read the back of one particular jar and tried not to let her curiosity show. "Oh, then don't tell me," she said, knowing full well the child would tell her, anyway.

"He said you looked like a skinny red lobster to him."

For the life of her, Maggie could not feign indifference to Nugget's statement. She looked at Nugget, her lips forming a thin, taut line as she pictured the child's imperious father. How she would like to take him down a notch or two, she silently fumed. It would be so satisfying to have him begging at her feet, but somehow she doubted that was a situation that would ever come about. Just why, she hadn't figured out yet.

"Oh, he did," she seethed. "Well, maybe your father needs a lesson in class and manners." She could tell him she'd had compliments on her beauty from far richer and more important men than him. In fact, some of her past admirers included a prince, a U.S. congressman and a famous film director. So what was one R.J. Buchanan's opinion? Absolutely nothing, she fumed silently.

Grabbing Nugget by the hand, she marched toward one of the checkout counters. The grim expression on her face did not alter, and Nugget looked up at her regretfully. "You're not mad at him, are you, Maggie? 'Cause I know he was only teasing. He said later that you had pretty eyes."

By now they had reached the cash register, and Maggie stepped into line behind an elderly man carrying a garden hose. While they waited, she looked down at Nugget suspiciously. "Are you just telling me this?" she demanded.

Nugget smiled widely now that she could see the anger fading from Maggie's face. "No. It's the truth, cross my heart. Ask him yourself," she suggested.

Maggie sighed and shook her head. "No, that's all right. It doesn't matter, anyway."

On the way home she kept telling herself those same words, but somehow the reasonable part of her brain just wasn't cooperating. And it made her furious to find the idea that R.J. thought she had pretty eyes pleased her. She shouldn't care what the man thought. But for some ridiculous reason unknown to her, she did.

Concentrating on cooking the evening meal took Maggie's complete attention, and in a short while she began to calm down. It wasn't so weird that she found herself attracted to a stranger. Why, it probably happened to women every day. And after she'd stayed there a couple of weeks and got to know the man, she would probably be laughing about the earlier fantasies he'd produced in her mind.

With Nugget's help, they had dinner ready by six o'clock. Maggie was hot and sweaty, her blouse splattered with grease and her hair a tumbled mess by then. Just before R.J. arrived, she almost changed her clothes and did something with her face, but she stopped herself. She was definitely not here to impress the man; she was only working as his housekeeper. She furiously told herself she didn't care what she looked like in front of him.

It was a quarter past when he pulled up in the jeep. Nugget ran out the kitchen door and Maggie looked through the window to see her just as she reached the jeep. The child was dancing around on her toes, obviously excited to have her dad back home.

Something clutched inside Maggie as she watched R.J. get out of the jeep, then stoop to enfold the little girl in his teak-brown arms. Nugget kissed his cheek enthusiastically, and he swung her up on his back piggyback-style and started toward the house.

Maggie scurried away from the window, afraid that he might catch her watching. She began washing a few dirty utensils and had her back to them when they entered the kitchen.

"Nugget tells me everything went all right today."

Maggie turned around at his voice, angry because the sound of it could affect her heartbeat. "Yes." She smiled. "It's been enlightening, to say the least."

He looked as though he'd been working very hard. He was wet with sweat, and there was some kind of fine white powder like dry cement or sawdust sticking to his clothes and deep brown skin.

"I'm sure." He grinned and Maggie dropped her eyes from his face. She had to. She felt that if she kept on looking at him he would surely see the forbidden thoughts running through her head.

"We've got supper all ready, Daddy," Nugget interrupted. "Hurry and wash. You've got to see how good it tastes."

His mustache moved in a dry little quirk as he looked from Maggie to Nugget. "I can't wait," he said and tossed his cap to Nugget as he walked out of the room.

Once they were all seated at the dinner table, Maggie began to wonder if she were suffering from some kind of mental disorder. She'd never had the problem of not being able to keep her eyes off a man before, and it was an urge she didn't know how to deal with. But he was so damned handsome! His hair was gorgeous, with dark brown curls waving and dipping thickly around his head. With it in view, he looked even more virile, and as Maggie studied him from beneath her lashes, words like *tough*, and *male*, and *sexy* kept running through her mind.

"We saw Darla today," Nugget told her dad as she began to cut through the skin of her baked potato. "She acted snooty to Maggie."

R.J. began to pile salad greens onto his plate, and Maggie watched with a puzzled frown. There was a salad bowl right in front of his plate. Why wasn't he using it?

"I'm sure Darla wasn't snooty. She doesn't even know Maggie," he reasoned in that smooth drawl of his, then looked up to see Maggie watching him. "What's the matter? Was she really snooty?"

The question caught Maggie off guard and she blushed beneath the frank gaze of his tawny eyes. "I, er, no," she lied. "I was just wondering why you weren't using your salad bowl."

He chuckled. "Out here, Maggie, we don't eat our meals in courses. We just eat. But don't worry, you're not socializing with someone who doesn't know proper etiquette. I just prefer to do it my way. Much to my mother's disgust, I might add."

Maggie's lips twisted wryly. "In other words, you're one of those people who defy convention."

He grinned as he sprinkled oil and vinegar over the salad. "In Texas, Miss Maggie, we call people like that outlaws. Is that what you consider me?"

His eyes lifted back up to her, and she met his gaze head-on. Their color and vivacity were electric, and she realized that he was a man who didn't bother to hide his feelings. Her soft lips curved into a smile. "That's rather a strong word to use just because a man doesn't use his salad bowl."

He laughed, and that thick dark mustache lifted to show those incredibly white teeth. "Yeah, but then you don't really know me, do you? After you've lived here awhile you may want to tag a name worse than that on me," he suggested.

Maggie shrugged and looked back down at her plate. For some reason there was a far too personal atmosphere suddenly building between them. She could feel it, but she couldn't understand why it was there.

"I'm not too worried," she murmured, feigning an interest in her food.

"Darla must have been worried," Nugget supplied between bites of potato. "When I told her Maggie was going to live with us, she looked kinda weird."

This time R.J. actually hooted. "I'll just bet she did," he said, then noticed Maggie's offended expression.

"Don't let it bother you, Maggie. Darla doesn't hold liberated views like you New York women do, that's all. Maybe you would call her narrow-minded."

Maggie looked at him coolly, her light blue eyes raking an icy path over his good-looking face. "No, I'd call her possessive." Right now she didn't care if she made him angry. She'd be damned if she'd let him sit there and categorize her with other women as if they were a herd of cows!

His brows met in a sardonic line to match the crooked grin of his mouth. She thought he was going to say something else, but then he turned his attention back to his food, as though she and her opinion didn't mean a flip to him.

Maggie began tackling the food on her plate, determined to put him out of her mind. She would act as if he wasn't even there. She would think about suave sophisticated Phillip and the praise he was always ready to bestow on her. Yes, there were men in the world with breeding; too bad this dark-haired devil had missed out.

"God Almighty! This thing is alive!"

The roar from R.J.'s end of the table brought Maggie out of her thoughts, and she stared at him as if he had gone completely mad.

"What's the matter?" Nugget asked easily, not at all intimidated by her father's outburst.

"This steak," he answered. "It's bleeding all over the plate."

"It's rare," Maggie said calmly.

He looked at her with sheer exasperation and shoved back his chair. "No, it's raw."

Maggie watched him carry his plate over to the stove. "I'm sorry. I didn't know how you liked your meat."

"I like it cooked," he quipped, plopping the steak back into the skillet.

Her mouth set in a tight, angry line, she left her seat and went over to the stove to join him. "Perhaps you can overlook it this time. Since I don't know you, I could hardly know how you like your steak."

"Forget it. Next time you'll know," he said in a somewhat softer tone as he adjusted the flame beneath the skillet.

"Are you always this temperamental?" She just had to ask.

He turned to look at her, his brows lifted in surprise, then suddenly he chuckled. "Why, Miss Maggie, I'm not temperamental. I'm just a man."

Maggie groaned inwardly at such a typical male statement. She would have liked to have said many things back to him, but for some reason she didn't. Instead, she surprised herself and him by asking, "Would you like me to finish cooking that for you?"

He looked at her for a moment, then shook his head. "No, just watch."

"Daddy's a good cook, Maggie. He can teach you lots of things," Nugget praised from across the table.

Maggie would enjoy teaching him a few things, too, she considered wryly. But the things running through her mind had absolutely nothing to do with food.

Chapter Five

Nugget, I'm going to feed the horses."

The child was helping Maggie do the dishes, but at the sound of her father's announcement she hastily plopped the saucer she was rinsing onto the drain board.

"Come on, Maggie, and see the horses," Nugget urged. "I want to show you mine. She's the prettiest one."

Maggie looked hesitantly from the child to R.J., who was waiting patiently by the door.

The invitation was tempting. Maggie rarely had the chance to be around horses and therefore had only ridden a few times in her life. She loved animals and had often thought of buying a few acres in upstate New York where she could keep a horse. Yet on the other hand, R.J. had her here to do the housework, not to mention that it would be safer all the way around if she did not get involved in family routines.

"Perhaps you should go on without me, Nugget. I need to finish the dishes," Maggie suggested.

From the corner of her eye, she could see an annoyed frown on R.J.'s face. "I'm not a slave driver, Maggie. I don't give a damn if the dishes are done. I hope you don't expect me to kill myself over your house, because I certainly don't intend to."

Maggie lifted her face to him. Actually she had forgotten that he was working for her, too. "No, of course not. But I—"

"Are you afraid of horses?"

"No, I adore them."

"Then quit fidgeting and come on."

Maggie hadn't thought she'd been fidgeting, but she hastily dried her hands on a dish towel and followed the two of them out the door.

Once she stepped out in the hot wind she realized how cool the air conditioner was keeping the interior of the house. The heat seemed to be blazing outside, even though it was probably seven-thirty by now.

"Do you have horses for a special reason?" Maggie asked as the three of them made their way toward the barn.

Nugget was skipping happily between her and R.J., sending up little puffs of dirt around her feet.

"Because I like them. That's really the only reason. I have raised and sold a few in the past for money, but not many. I get too attached to them and don't want to give them up."

Maggie studied him thoughtfully. It surprised her to hear him admit he could get attached to something. Most men thought that was an unmacho trait. But maybe Mr. Buchanan was so confident of his masculinity that he never felt threatened by anything.

"Then you've had more than this at one time?"

He nodded. "I had as many as ten at one time."

R.J. didn't need to whistle for the horses. Once they caught sight of him, they all came trotting toward the wooden feed troughs, hungry nickers issuing from their velvety mouths.

"Mine is the blue dappled one," Nugget proudly told her. "Her name is Powder Puff and she's real nice. She never kicks or bites."

"It is nice not to have those habits," Maggie said with a laugh.

She and Nugget stood by the iron-pipe fence while R.J. spread a mixture of grain in the feed troughs. The horses nuzzled him fondly and he stroked them, giving each one a special greeting.

"What are the names of the other horses?" Maggie asked.

"The black one is Beau," Nugget answered, pointing out a heavily muscled horse. "The red one is Maybelline, and her baby is Bell. Then the paint is Windsong, and her baby is Choya—like the cactus. Do you know how to ride, Maggie?" she asked, looking eagerly up at Maggie.

Maggie leaned against the fence. "Just enough to stay on," she admitted. "Perhaps if we have the time you can teach me?"

This suggestion thrilled Nugget, and the child yelled over to her father as she danced on the toes of her tennis shoes.

"Maggie wants me to teach her how to ride. Doesn't that sound fun, Daddy?"

By now R.J. was finished with the feed and as he walked toward Maggie and Nugget, he folded the empty grain sack and tossed it into a black barrel sitting by the fence. "Sounds like fun for you, Nugget. I don't know about Maggie, though," he added wryly. Humor glinted in his eyes as he looked her way. "Do you know anything about riding?"

"Just which side you mount and dismount on and how to hold the reins. I've ridden a little, but that was a long time ago."

"I don't suppose the modeling profession has a need for horseback riders," he mused.

Maggie's lips curved into a soft smile at his assumption. "No, but occasionally there are horses used in the background. It depends on the item being advertised."

"Uncle George showed us a picture in a magazine once where you were advertising lipstick. Your lips looked gorgeous, Maggie. Didn't they, Daddy?"

R.J. grinned broadly. "They looked so pretty I almost kissed the picture," he admitted in mock seriousness.

Nugget giggled. "Oh, you didn't, either!"

Maggie laughed, too, at the idea of this tough-looking man kissing a piece of paper. Yet when he looked across to Maggie and his eyes lingered on her mouth, her laughter suddenly died and she had to look away. It was the first time he'd come close to looking at her as a woman, and for some reason she felt frightened.

"Can I fill the water trough?" Nugget asked, already scooting under the fence and heading toward the barn, as if she knew the answer.

"Be sure to turn the faucet off," he called after his daughter's retreating back.

Maggie's eyes followed Nugget, but she could feel R.J. watching her and she shifted restlessly then turned to look at him.

"I . . . Nugget said her parents were killed. It's amazing how normal and well adjusted she is," Maggie told him.

He leaned against the fence, the fingers of one hand hooked lazily in the pocket of his jeans.

"I'll take that as a compliment, Maggie. Since I've raised her from the time she was fifteen months old—a baby, really." He sighed, and then, looking out over the barren landscape, he continued with a soft chuckle. "I was twenty-six when I became a substitute father. We had to grow up together. You can imagine what a young single male knows about raising a baby girl. Believe me, at times it's been very comical."

Maggie smiled, her blue eyes sliding over his relaxed body. God, what a mixture he was! He was nothing, absolutely nothing, like the men she knew. "So Nugget doesn't remember her parents at all?" she asked.

"No. Her father was my twin brother."

Maggie's lips parted in astonishment. So that was why Nugget looked so much like him! "Oh, I'm sorry. Would it be prying to ask what happened?"

He shrugged, as though to tell her the initial pain of it had worn off long ago. "James was a lawyer like our father. He practiced in my father's firm down in Corpus Christi. He and his wife, Gayla, had flown up here for a weekend visit. You see, I'm the black sheep. I was supposed to have been a lawyer, too, but I shook the whole Buchanan family tree when I changed my major from law to engineering. James didn't hold it against me, though. We were close and kept in constant touch. He and Gayla would come up here often to get away from clients and the whirlwind social life of the city. James owned his own Cessna and was a good pilot, but a few minutes after he took off from Amarillo the engine failed. The plane dived into some power lines and set off an explosion."

Maggie found her fingers were literally clenched to the fence post, and she tried to swallow down the horror that was suddenly choking her.

"What about Nugget? She wasn't in the plane?"

R.J. shook his head. "They had left her in the care of our parents back in Corpus Christi."

For a moment, the only sound around them was the horses munching grain and stomping the pestering flies at their heels, and in the background the whisper of the neverending wind. These sounds registered absently on Maggie's senses as she tried to imagine this man losing his brother, a brother who had literally developed beside him in his mother's womb. It was too tragic even to contemplate. But obviously this man had had to face it.

"How did you happen to take over the parenting of Nugget? Weren't there other relatives?"

"Gayla didn't have any relatives to speak of, and my parents are not exactly the type to raise a baby." R.J.'s mouth twisted wryly as his eyes expressed a reflective mood. "James and I were like arms and legs to each other. He wouldn't have wanted anyone to raise his child but me. You see, I knew this even before their death."

Maggie's brows lifted in puzzlement, and he went on. "On our twenty-sixth birthday, James called me from the law office. He said, "Brother, in honor of our birthday, I'm making myself a will, and you're included. I laughed and told him he didn't have anything I needed; I had all I wanted up here on the caprock. We laughed and joked for a few minutes, and then he said, "R.J., if something ever happened to Gayla and me, would you take Emmaline and raise her as your own?" God, I thought he was crazy at the time. A young man, fresh out of law school, with a beautiful wife and daughter and the world ahead of him, was worried about making a will. I told him sure, but that he shouldn't be worrying about dying from social stress just yet. I took it all so lightly.

"No one knows what lies ahead," Maggie murmured philosophically.

R.J. straightened and shifted so that his arms rested across the top rail of the fence. "James and Gayla's death taught me that in one shattering moment."

He was looking out over the fence, watching Nugget in the distance as she squirted the hose playfully into the horse's water trough. Maggie studied his profile, wondering how he had reacted at the time of the accident. Strong was the only thing she could imagine him being.

"Does that mean you took life for granted before?"

He turned to look at her. Gone was the teasing mischief that had sparkled earlier in his eyes; now they were clouded with gravity. "I think everyone does at one time or another. But as for Nugget—it's like she was conceived from me, also, and she came to me at a time when my life might have headed down a back road. I like to think I was put here for her and she for me.''

In the past years, Maggie had feared she was growing insensitive. She often wondered if she was even becoming callous toward other people's plights. She didn't know if it was from living in a large, tough city, or from grinding out a career in a profession where back stabbing was as natural as breathing. Right at this moment, it didn't matter what the reason was. R.J.'s words had actually brought a mist of tears to her eyes, and for the first time since she was a child she felt embarrassed at being moved by a sad, even though true, story. Even more confusing was the idea that if a man back in New York had told her the very same words, she would have appeared outwardly sympathetic, but on the inside she would have thought, God, how maudlin!

What was it, her mind frantically screamed. Was it this heat, this barren, wind-clawed land that made everything so raw and open, this man before her so earthy and real? Maggie didn't know, but she did know that R. J. Buchanan was affecting her far too much for her own well-being. She had only known him for a matter of twenty-four hours, yet already she knew it would disturb her greatly if she thought tomorrow would be her last time to see him. What had she done by coming out here? Gone from one cloying situation to one that could prove to be profoundly more dangerous?

''Maggie, do you take your modeling job as seriously as you seem to be this housekeeping thing? It's nine o'clock. Why don't you sit down and have a beer with me?''

R.J. tossed the paper he had been reading to one side as he watched Maggie move the oiled dust rag over the top of the television.

Maggie lifted the rag and turned to look at him. ''That's all right—I don't like beer, or at least I don't think I do.''

"What does that mean?" he wanted to know, reaching for the can of Lone Star positioned on the floor by his armchair.

He must be a Texan through and through, she mused. He even drank beer that was brewed right in the state. "I've never drunk beer before," she admitted.

His mouth twisted into a wry grin. "No, you would be more the Chablis type, wouldn't you?" He held the can from which he had been drinking toward Maggie. "Here, try mine. You might actually like it. And I think that while you're living in Texas, you'll appreciate anything that's cooling."

She looked at his almost taunting expression and then at the can, which had droplets of condensed moisture on the sides. Shrugging she walked across the room to him. "Why not?" she said with a little smile. "After all, I'm not in New York, am I?"

His tawny eyes narrowed slightly as she took the can from his fingers. "No, there's no one here you need to impress."

Her brows lifted to an indignant arch. "Is that what you think I do, Mr. Buchanan? Try to impress people?" she asked coolly.

A quirk of a grin moved his lips. "I thought that's what models were paid to do. To urge people to look, to reach out and touch, to buy."

The last words were spoken softly as he settled back in his chair, but the glitter in his eyes belied the relaxed position.

"In other words, you think a model is a solicitant," she commented haughtily.

He chuckled at her offended attitude. "My, my, Maggie, how your mind runs in the gutters."

"You implied—" she countered.

"No, you jumped to conclusions. I merely meant that a model is an instrument to sell items, nothing more. And we both know that to do that, a person needs to be impressive."

He grinned at her, rather impishly she thought, and she could not stop herself from smiling, too.

"Maybe you're right," she said, taking the matching armchair next to his. "You just make it sound so unglamorous."

His mouth twisted wryly as he slid his eyes over Maggie. "And that's important to you, being glamorous?"

"Naturally," she answered, crossing her legs and lifting the beer can to her lips. She tried not to think that his lips had touched the same spot. "There's not a woman who exists who doesn't love a little glamor."

He watched her taste the beer with a bland expression, then asked, "What do you think?"

Maggie thoughtfully licked the yeasty brew from her lips. "It's rather nice—nothing like I expected." Like him, she thought. Nothing similar to her notion of the male of the species.

R.J. got up from the chair and went through to the kitchen. In his absence, Maggie leaned her head back against the chair. She was tired, she realized, and it was going to be wonderful to sleep in a real bed tonight instead of on an air mattress. Nugget had gone to bed almost an hour ago, and she wondered if the little girl usually retired so early in the evening.

Her thoughts were interrupted as R.J. reappeared, standing in front of her with a cut-glass goblet filled with beer.

"Maybe this will make you feel more at home," he suggested, handing her the glass.

Maggie took it from him, sipping it as she watched him sink into his armchair. The beer was refreshing, but for some reason she wished he had not made the gesture of pouring it into this elegant glass. It made her different from him, and she didn't want that. She wished she could ask him not to treat her differently. *I can do the things you do, speak the same language you speak,* she thought resentfully. But that wouldn't be entirely right, she had to admit. Their respective lives might have taken place at opposite ends of the earth. Her friends back in New York wouldn't drink beer out of a can. They wouldn't drink beer at all.

"Does Nugget usually go to bed so early?" she asked after several minutes had passed in silence.

R.J. shook his head as he lazily crossed his feet in front of him. "No, but I suppose the excitement of having you here has worn her down. Usually she doesn't hit bed until ten."

Maggie studied him from beneath her lowered lashes. He wasn't sitting in the armchair as a normal person would. He was half lying in it, his back resting against the bottom cushion. He was shirtless, and the sight of him so relaxed irritated Maggie no end. Didn't he know the sight of him was distracting her away from all common sense?

"Did you know that isn't good for your spinal column?"

"I've never heard of beer hurting anyone's back before," he answered lazily.

One of Maggie's legs swung in nervous agitation. "Not the beer! The way you're sitting, or lying, or whatever it is you're doing."

"Says who?"

Maggie let out a breath impatiently. "Say the health professionals. Didn't your mother teach you to sit with good posture?"

His lips moved slowly into a grin as brown eyes danced with amusement. "Sure, but good posture doesn't feel good."

Maggie digested his words without any surprise at all. "And you always do what feels good," she stated knowingly.

He chuckled. "Yeah—remember, I'm a real outlaw," he drawled. "No salad bowl, bad posture, beer out of a can. Before you learn any more bad things about me, I'll just

come out and tell you. I'm a man of the senses. See, taste
and touch.''

Maggie had to look away from his laughing eyes, and she
swallowed before asking, "In that order?"

"No, sometimes I smell first."

Even though he spoke in amusement, Maggie found the
words somehow suggestive, and she looked away from him
to stare down at the amber liquid in her glass. It was strange
that she should read sexual implications in all he said and
did. Phillip or any of her men acquaintances could say out-
right lewd things and they rolled off her back. So why did
R.J.'s simple words make her whole body feel flushed?

"You like the beer?" he asked, breaking the silence.

Maggie looked at him, and it came as a shock to know her
eyes and mind had already memorized the strong lines of his
face and the deep sable color of his hair and mustache.

"I think it's something that could grow on me," she finally answered.

Several hours later, Maggie sat up on the side of the bed,
her fingers pushing tiredly at her tousled hair. She had
tossed on the bed for what seemed like ages, and she could
bear the confines of it no longer.

With the lights out and the house in total quiet except for
the hum of the air conditioner, Maggie had too much of an
opportunity to think, and that was the one thing she didn't
want to do. But she had to keep asking herself just what she
was doing there in a stranger's house.

She had never been an impulsive person before. However, during the past month it seemed she had been doing
nothing but taking rash, impulsive steps. Why? She was
overwhelmingly wealthy with a fabulous career, a beautiful
apartment in a well-to-do part of New York City. Why then
was she here in the Texas desert, keeping house for a man
and child whom she didn't even know existed before yesterday?

Phillip, her parents, her friends, everyone who had thought her insane to even contemplate coming out here in the first place would believe her to be truly mad at this new undertaking.

But how much did she really care about what they thought? Hadn't she spent most of her life trying to please someone else? Her parents, Phillip, and yes, even Mario. Wasn't it time she did something for herself and on her own without someone looking over her shoulder, directing her this way or that way, prodding her to make the correct decision?

She knew the answer had to be yes. But the doubts that assailed her now were those about whether her decision had been the right one. In any other circumstance, she would have said yes, but now, as she thought of R.J. lying across the hall in his bed, she felt very unsure. He did things to her, things he was totally unaware of, and things that no one had ever managed before and it made her very wary of the time looming ahead of her. He had said he was a man of the senses. Maybe that was why he awakened every one of Maggie's senses until she was tingling with awareness.

Sighing, she rose from the bed and pulled a crinkled cotton robe over her body. She wasn't accustomed to going to bed so early. Ten o'clock was like the middle of the day for a New Yorker, and Maggie had always been a night person. Anyway, how was she supposed to sleep without any traffic rushing below her windows? Was the creak of the incessant wind supposed to take the place of honking horns?

Desperate with restlessness, she padded barefoot to the living room, careful to walk lightly in case she might wake Nugget or R.J.

Moonlight was slanting through the picture window and allowed Maggie to see her way. Her purse was hidden away on top of the refrigerator and she pulled it down and fished out a packet of cigarettes and the lighter R.J. had used to light the pilots. Maybe a cigarette would ease her tension.

She could go out on the back patio so that the smoke wouldn't awaken anyone. That and some fresh air should do the trick, she thought.

As she went outside, Maggie was startled to find it was still very hot. The sun had been down for hours, yet the wind was as warm as if it was blowing off an oven.

There was a grouping of outdoor furniture on the patio next to the pool. The dark rust-and-yellow print of the cushions was now muted with the silvery darkness. Maggie sank onto the chaise longue with an audible sigh and proceeded to light a cigarette.

She had taken perhaps three draws on it when she heard footsteps behind her.

Turning her head, she watched R.J. halt beside her chair. He studied her for a moment, then asked, "Couldn't you sleep?"

When Maggie shook her head, he added, "I didn't know you smoked."

Utterly surprised by the distaste in his voice, she turned wide eyes upon him. "Sometimes I do. Why? Does it offend you?"

"It's not me I'm concerned about. It's Nugget. I have a feeling you're going to become a big example for her in the coming weeks."

Maggie frowned impatiently and reached to stub out her cigarette. "And you think that by seeing me smoke she'll want to do it sometime in the future? Come on, isn't that a little too much?"

R.J. took a deep breath as though he was fast losing his temper. "I don't want you smoking around Nugget. Maybe I can't expect you to understand this. You're not a parent yet. But someday when you are, you'll understand how I feel."

Indignation swept through Maggie. Other than Phillip, no man had ever told her what she could and couldn't do, and she viewed R.J.'s actions as overbearing, to say the least.

"No, perhaps I don't understand. But I do have the capacity to know that you can't shield your daughter from everything that crosses her path," she reasoned, her voice rising with irritation.

"I totally agree," he responded with a voice so smooth that it prickled the hairs on the back of Maggie's neck.

"Besides," she went on, feeling a definite need to defend herself. "I think you just like being dictatorial."

She sensed more than heard him take the chair next to her, but she didn't turn to look at him. She felt degraded and hurt for some reason. This man had no right to interfere with her personal preferences or habits. No right at all!

"Have you ever seen anyone die of cancer, Maggie?" he asked after a few moments of tense silence had passed.

She shook her head, expecting to hear a long speech against the evils of cigarette smoking.

"Well, I have, and it's ugly. I wouldn't want to see it happen to a young, lovely thing like you."

Maggie swallowed and found her hands were clenched on the arms of the chair. His words jolted her. Not because he had used the words *death* or *cancer*. No, she had instantly assumed he was trying to play macho man with her. But the concern in his voice made a mockery of her assumption.

"If you had warned me you disliked cigarettes so much, I certainly wouldn't have smoked. I...I just couldn't sleep—" What was wrong with her? Here she was stuttering and stammering as if she was the one who had been in the wrong, while he was the one who had been offensive, even if his motivation had been one of concern.

His sigh was audible on the wind, and she turned to look at him as he said, "Forget it, Maggie. I...it just angers me to see anybody abusing their body. Look," he went on before she could respond, "if you want to back out now, it's all right with me. I won't hold you to any oral contract."

Maggie stared at him in the silvery darkness. What had Nugget called him? Moonlight Bandit? Well, the name couldn't have been more fitting. With nothing on but jeans and boots and his almost black hair tousled around his face, he could have been one of the cowboy bandits that roamed and pillaged this wild country before sheriffs and the Texas Rangers had brought law and order to the land.

"Do you want me to leave?" she asked and was amazed to find her hands trembling as she waited for his answer. It was frightening to admit to herself just how much she wanted to stay.

He shrugged and leaned back in the chair. "No, I still need someone, but you may not want to live by my standards. In two more days you might be cursing this place and crying for New York. You haven't failed to notice there *is* a big difference?"

"I would have been blind not to have noticed," she replied.

"And you still want to stay?"

Did she? Did she really want to stay and take the chance of having her heart twisted out of shape? Because something in the back of her mind warned her that to stay here just might mean that. Yet the question was merely superfluous because, in a way, he had already made up her mind without even trying.

"Yes."

The word was huskily spoken, but when R.J. spoke, his voice was crisp and businesslike. "Good, because I would hate for Nugget to get attached to you and then have you pull up stakes on us."

So he was thinking of Nugget. And Maggie was thinking of him. "Whatever you may think of me, Mr. Buchanan, I always stick to my commitments once I've made them."

He studied her for a moment and then suddenly smiled. "Good," he drawled and then reached for her hand to pull her to her feet. "Don't you think we'd better go back in? We've both got work to do tomorrow."

As Maggie felt the rough, callused skin of his hand against hers, she couldn't think about the work she would be doing tomorrow. She could only think how thrilled she was that she would be seeing him tomorrow, and the next day, and the next....

Chapter Six

The sound of running water woke Maggie the next morning. At first she was so disoriented that she thought it was raining outside. Then she remembered where she was, and she knew it wasn't rain. She was in Texas. It probably never rained in this place!

She moaned at the thought and rolled over to press her face into the pillow. If that incessant noise would stop, maybe she could go back to sleep. She was tired. It had taken forever to go to sleep and even then she had dreamed.... As her thoughts became clearer, she sat bolt upright in bed. The sound was distinguishable now. It was the shower running. She was in bed, and R.J. was already showering. Oh, why hadn't she had the sense to set an alarm clock!

Taking only the time to throw on her robe and slippers, she rushed into the kitchen. Once there, she stared around her in blank panic. What should she do first? It would probably be only a matter of a few moments before R.J. walked in, ready for his breakfast.

Gathering her wits together, she began to fill the percolator with cold water. Why couldn't the man open a can of breakfast drink for his morning meal? Or have a doughnut and glass of orange juice? Because he was a man who worked, her mind answered as she began to spread bacon in a skillet. He wasn't like most of the men she knew who sat behind an executive's desk or ran here and there to board meetings, or met a client over cocktails. R.J. got out and really labored beneath the hot sun. His body would demand food. Maybe that was why she had first noticed him. There was a wholesomeness about him that was not contrived by clothes or hairstyles. No, there was nothing glittery or plastic about R. J. Buchanan.

Most of the food was well on its way to being done by the time R.J. did appear in the kitchen. As he greeted her, Maggie turned away from the stove to look at him. She couldn't have known that he had been standing there for a few moments watching her movements as she placed strips of bacon on a paper towel.

Maggie stared in complete surprise. All her earlier assumptions were quickly squashed as she took in the sight of his gray summer suit, and his dexterous movements as he pushed the knot of his tie into place.

"You're going to work in that!" she exclaimed in spite of herself.

"Mmm." He shrugged, completely unaffected by her dismay. "I have a meeting with a few municipal people this morning. The Department of Human Services is needing a new wing of offices. I think they've accepted my bid."

"Oh," she said. Apparently there was more to this man than she knew. "Well, I hope you don't mind waiting a minute or two. I didn't wake up quite as early as I had planned to."

He smiled lazily at her and strolled into the room. "There's no need to rush. Remember, I'm the boss."

Her lips slanted into a wry smile, but inside her stomach was doing silly little somersaults. He looked so fresh, so male and so handsome. His hair was shiny and black with water and combed away from his forehead. He was freshly shaven, and the sultry smell of spices emanated from his clothes and skin.

"Besides," he went on, "I really didn't intend you to cook three meals a day. I can do breakfast. I've been doing it since I was eighteen and went off to college."

Maggie turned back to the stove and took a deep breath. Just looking at the man made her feel shaky! What would happen if he did actually kiss her? Determinedly, she jerked her mind away from the thought.

"When I take on something, I want to go the whole way with it," she told him. Then she added in a teasing tone, "Don't worry, breakfast is the one meal I can cook. I learned to do that because sometimes when I'm not on a job I like to be lazy and eat breakfast."

He stood beside her and picked up a piece of bacon from the paper towel. "You don't have live-in help?" he asked, biting into the crisp meat.

Maggie shook her head. "Not now, since I live by myself. My schedule is too varied. Sometimes I'm gone for weeks running, so I just have someone come in every few days to do the cleaning."

He finished the bacon and reached for another piece, grinning mischievously when Maggie gave him a reproving look. "You live right in New York City?" he wanted to know. She nodded and he asked, "You like it?"

One of Maggie's shoulders lifted in a shrug as she contemplated his question. She had never given it serious thought before. In fact, no one had ever bothered to ask her if she liked living in the city. No one she knew would consider living anywhere else.

"I suppose I do. But then that's hard to answer. You see, the city is what I've always known. I've never lived anywhere else," she admitted.

He left her to pour himself a cup of coffee. Once he had it in hand, he sat at the table and waited for Maggie to finish with the food.

When the meal was ready, she started to pull out a chair and join him, then suddenly remembered Nugget. "Shall I wake Nugget for breakfast?"

R.J. shook his head. "Let her sleep. She doesn't mind eating cold food."

He should know, Maggie thought, as she sat across from him. It still boggled her mind to think of a single man raising a baby, but obviously R.J. had done it and done it well.

She began filling her plate, thinking she shouldn't be eating like this. But the food smelled so appetizing and she found she was ravenous. Phillip would be furious if she put on a pound while she was here, but on the other hand, R.J. had called her skinny. The comment still rankled, even though she told herself that since R.J. knew nothing of the fashion business, he couldn't know that being thin was a necessity, not necessarily something she wanted.

"You mentioned going to college. How did you decide to become an engineer?" Maggie asked. It was ridiculous how curious she was about this man. She hoped he wouldn't notice.

"I found that building things was a lot more interesting than trying to prove a point that in the end wouldn't change a thing, anyway. While my brother was reading law books, I started using a hammer and nails. When I was twelve, I built my mother a cedar chest, and that's all it took. She cherished it and it held her most beloved possessions. I got such a worthwhile feeling from my mother's reaction that I knew I wanted to build bigger and better things, things with walls where people would live and make their homes; rooms where lives would change and grow. I've never lost that feeling. I hope I never do.''

''Since your father came from a long line of lawyers, how did he take your decision to become an engineer?''

''Not as badly as I expected. When we were in college, James's major was always discussed among friends, and mine was treated like leprosy.''

The last he grunted with amusement, and Maggie's blue eyes widened on him curiously. How could he take such treatment so lightly? Surely it must have been painful to have his brother gloated over while he was considered inferior just because he had chosen a different direction. ''Didn't that bother you?'' she asked, a bit dismayed.

''Hell, no,'' he chuckled. ''I thought it was funny.''

She frowned at this. ''So you did it partly to thwart your father,'' she stated in reproach.

His eyebrows went up at this with amused surprise. ''Not at all. Do I really look that stupid? As far as my career goes, I've always been purely selfish. I did it because I wanted to do it and was good at it, to boot.''

''Did you and your father become estranged because of your decision?''

He bit into a piece of buttered toast before answering. ''No,'' he replied, as if her question was ridiculous. ''I'm not that narrow-minded and grudges are senseless. I just tried to recognize him for what he was, and if he doesn't understand me—well, that's not what I consider an earth-shattering problem. Nugget needing braces, or going out with the right boy on her sixteenth birthday is much more important to me.''

He grinned at her as he lifted his coffee cup to his lips and his tawny-colored eyes roamed Maggie's face. In that instant she knew he really meant what he said and found she liked him for it.

''You're just too happy.'' She smiled back and then giggled at her next thoughts. ''You're supposed to have psychological hang-ups because you were a twin. Everyone knows twins have unusual jealousies of each other. They obsessively vie for their parents love and attention. You should even have a repressed personality because your father didn't encourage your interests while he indulged your brother's. You really should see a therapist. After all that, anyone as happy as you are can't be healthy."

He laughed and then suddenly he looked at her, his eyes a bit too intent for her comfort. "What about you, Maggie Winslow? Are you a happy person?"

Her eyes swiftly dropped to her plate. "I've never thought about it," she said. It was the truth, she realized. She had always been too busy to ever wonder if she was really happy. She only knew when things were going well or not going so well.

"That sounds rather stupid," he said, watching her fumble with her fork as she pretended an interest in the scrambled egg on her plate.

"Perhaps," she admitted, lifting her head to smile up at him. "But Phillip doesn't give me time to think about such things. And when I'm working, that consumes all my thoughts."

"Who's Phillip?" he asked.

"My agent."

He drained the last of his coffee and rose from the table. "Well, Maggie, it sounds to me like you need to get rid of this Phillip."

In the world of fashion, dropping Phillip Saville as an agent would be like cutting one's own throat. The idea was amusing, to say the least!

"I'm afraid that's impossible," she told him.

He shrugged as though he wouldn't find anything impossible. "Then all I can say is I'm glad I'm my own agent." He grinned.

Maggie watched him stroll across the room to pick up an extra set of work clothes from the window seat. He was the perfect image of carefree, self-assured contentment, and she almost hated him for it because she wished fervently that she could be just like him.

"I'd better be moving," he said, glancing at the watch on his wrist and starting toward the door. "Don't bother with supper. I play softball tonight, so we'll grab a hamburger in town."

She wondered if that included her, too, but didn't ask. After all, she didn't want to appear presumptuous, and it would be embarrassing if he was planning to take a girl-friend along.

"By the way," he added, winking at her as he stepped out the door. "You were right about one thing. You do know how to cook breakfast."

She smiled at him before the door shut him from view. Turning back to her plate, she wished his parting words hadn't made her feel so good. It was stupid of her! Absolutely foolish!

"Maggie, what are you doing?" Nugget asked, aghast, her brown eyes disbelieving as she looked at Maggie's fingers plunged into a bowl of polish remover.

"I'm taking off my fingernails, that's what," she answered impatiently, lifting her left hand out to see if the false tips had loosened from her real nails.

"But why?" the child wanted to know. "They're so beautiful!"

Maggie sighed at Nugget's exclamation. "They don't look beautiful with four of them broken off at the quick!"

There was no use trying to save the rest of them, she thought angrily. By the time she did a few more loads of clothes tomorrow and another sinkful of dishes, they would all be broken, anyway.

"But you haven't changed your clothes yet, and if you don't hurry Daddy will be here."

"So?" Maggie returned. "There's no need for me to cook. He's taking you for a hamburger because tonight is his ball night or something like that."

Nugget shook her little blond head and stuck one thonged foot out in front of the other with an impatient twist to her hips. "I know. But you're supposed to be ready, too."

Maggie looked a bit closer at the girl. "I'm not going. I wasn't invited. Your daddy is probably taking a girlfriend, and I would only be in the way."

Nugget giggled at this. "Silly, Daddy never takes a girl-friend to his ball games. He always takes them dancing or something mushy like that."

Maggie digested this information with mixed feelings. She didn't know if she would rather be one of the girls he took dancing or the one going to the ball game.

"I'll...I'll see when your dad gets home," Maggie said, then went on before Nugget could make another protest, "Now, can you help me get the rest of these things off my nails?"

By the time R.J. did make it home, Maggie was dressed in aqua-colored jogging shorts and a white T-shirt with a coordinating tropical print on the back. Her feet were en-cased in white anklets and tennis shoes, and one foot was swinging nervously back and forth as she sat at the dressing table in her bedroom.

As she smoothed clear polish over her nails, Maggie heard the sound of R.J.'s jeep arrive. Nugget's chatter was clear as he entered the house.

"Are you girls ready?" As the sound of their footsteps grew louder in the hallway, Maggie could hear him speak-ing to Nugget.

"I am, but Maggie says she isn't going," Nugget's petu-lant voice replied.

Maggie grimaced, wondering what R.J. was thinking at this moment. She wasn't long in finding out. The next moment he entered her bedroom, looking at her with a hard expression on his face.

"What's the matter? Is a baseball game not refined enough for you?"

The drawl of his voice had hardened to that of a complete stranger, and she thought that maybe he'd made the wrong career choice. A voice like that would be perfect for a prosecuting attorney.

"No," she blurted and then shook her head. "I...I mean this is obviously a family affair, and since I'm not even a friend I don't want to intrude—"

"Hellfire," he barked. "What do you mean, not a friend? What does it take to be your friend? You're living in my house, aren't you? What is it with you? Do you have to pay people in New York to be your friend, make them pass some kind of mental and social test before you can say he's my friend?"

Inwardly she cringed, for his anger affected her far too much. She had made people angry at her before and never once thought about it. She didn't know why *he* should be any different, but he was. She wanted to receive his smiles, his kind words, his approval, and her eyes widened on him with something like awe as she realized how dangerous that kind of thinking could be for her.

"No—it's not like that," she said. "It's just that, well, you hired me as your housekeeper—"

"Well," he interrupted in a sarcastic tone, "you contracted me to remodel your house. Does that mean we can't treat each other like friends?"

She shook her head as he stood looking at her, one booted foot out in front of him, his shirt sweaty and dusty.

"No," she reasoned, then met his gaze and smiled, realizing how senseless this argument was. "And I would like to go very much. I...I've never been to a softball game before."

She could see the anger drain out of him and he grinned at her, his amber-colored eyes lit with their usual humor. "Then I'd better play well tonight, hadn't I?"

Maggie nodded and he started toward the door. When he reached it, he turned to add, "And, Maggie, as long as you're here, you are part of the family."

"Thank you," she murmured, finding it impossible to hold his gaze. His words and expression were suddenly too intimate, and she didn't know how to handle the situation. The idea made her want to laugh hysterically. Imagine Maggie Winslow, the woman who had once dated a prince, not being able to handle a few kind words from a Texas construction engineer. Lord, she thought humorlessly, she must be slipping!

A few minutes later, they were in R.J.'s white Mustang convertible headed toward Amarillo. Maggie was in the bucket seat next to R.J., and Nugget was in the back sitting on the edge of the seat so that she could keep her head between the two adults.

Since the top was down, Maggie's long hair was blowing wildly around her face. For several miles she struggled with it, but finally she was forced to get a ribbon from her purse and tie it away from her face.

As she fretted with the ribbon, R.J. shocked her by saying, "Your hair is beautiful, Maggie, but maybe while you're here it would be cooler if you cut it."

Maggie looked at him as if he had gone mad. "I couldn't do that!" she exclaimed as she finished tying the ribbon. "Phillip would kill me."

He tossed her a bored look. "Does Phillip tell you when to use the bathroom?"

Maggie's cheeks reddened at this. "Remember, I'm a model," she retorted. "And because Phillip is my agent he virtually controls my appearance."

His lips slanted to a sardonic twist. "That must be great fun."

Maggie shrugged, not wanting to admit just what a bore it had become the past year or so. "It's something I've learned to live with."

His reply was only a grunt of disapproval, and Maggie unconsciously touched her hand to her hair. It surprised her greatly that R.J. had even noticed it.

"Look at Maggie's hands, Daddy," Nugget said. "She took off her fingernails."

Maggie wanted to slither down in the floorboard as R.J. took his eyes off the highway to glance at her hands, lying loosely in her lap.

To her further dismay, he reached over and picked up her left one, a crooked grin on his mouth as he studied the short nails with clear varnish shining them.

"I thought the long ones were pretty," Nugget said, "but Maggie said they weren't for doing dishes. What do you think, Daddy?"

"I think this is a hand I could hold."

Maggie's cheeks grew warm as Nugget giggled and R.J.'s hard fingers curved around hers.

"I held hands with a boy at school once," Nugget proudly interjected.

"Oh?" R.J. grinned, glancing back at the child's animated face. "How did you like it?"

Nugget shrugged and wiggled around on the seat. Maggie felt like wiggling, also. Her hand being captured in R.J.'s was unsettling, to say the least.

"It was okay," Nugget answered in all seriousness. "But it was pretty hard to eat lunch with my left hand. And his fingers kept getting mine sticky and sweaty."

R.J. laughed at the girl's summation. "That can happen," he told his daughter, and then his laughing eyes looked down at his and Maggie's clasped hands. "So maybe I'd better let go of Maggie's before that happens to us."

When he released her hand, Maggie was surprised to find that instead of feeling relieved, she suddenly felt bereft. She told herself she was fast losing her senses. Holding hands with a man! She needed to be back in New York. Heaven help her, she'd never think of holding a man's hand there. The idea was ludicrous and the thought had her lips twisting to a wry line as she stared down at her hands. She hadn't seen her fingers manicured in such a way since she was a very young teenager. Her hands were slender but the fingers were not skinny. With sculptured nails they looked long and graceful—very chic. In New York, she would never have gone anywhere with her hands like this. But R.J. had said he liked her own real fingernails instead of the long fake ones. The thought made her unusually happy and softened the line of her lips to a little smile. Her looks had been contrived for so long that she wondered just where the real Maggie started and ended; in a tiny way, R.J. had just shown her.

She cast a surreptitious glance across at R.J. His strong hands loosely gripped the steering wheel, the wind played with the dark curls at the edge of his cap and his eyes were shaded by wire-framed sunglasses. When she'd first seen him at Tony's, she had considered him attractive, but coarse, perhaps even ignorant. It was startling to realize how wrong she'd been and how her feelings had changed so swiftly.

She looked at her hands once again, her thoughts suddenly swerving. Phillip wouldn't like her hands like this. He wouldn't see their natural beauty. She could already hear him ripping her apart with that jeering voice he could so easily employ. Do you think anyone wants to see a model with hands that look like they've been changing a dozen diapers!

Maggie's spirits dimmed as thoughts of Phillip reminded her she would be going back after a few weeks. The sculptured nails would return, her sunburn would be gone, her hair would be conditioned back into shape from this dry environment. She would look beautiful again—contrived, but beautiful. Why didn't the idea please her? Why did her career seem even more stifling since she had met this moonlight bandit with laughing brown eyes?

The ballpark was a small one located in one of the city's parks. Nugget insisted that she and Maggie sit behind home plate. Several yards behind them were a few scraggly elm trees, but their shade did not provide much protection from the hot sun. Maggie was sure she would be broiled alive, but after the game got under way she totally forgot the heat.

Even though the teams had only matching T-shirts for uniforms and the players ranged from teenagers to the middle-aged, they all played with high spirits and determination to win. The spectators were just as exuberant, and Maggie thought to herself that she could well have been watching a game between the New York Mets and the L.A. Dodgers. The shouts and claps never stopped, and she even found herself yelling encouragement to R.J. each time he went to bat.

Maggie wasn't surprised to see that he was a good athlete. He played third base flawlessly, throwing several batters out and smashing just as many hits into the outfield. However, his efforts weren't enough to pull them ahead of the opposing team. When the last inning was over, his team had lost five to three, but from the grin on R.J.'s sweating face, no one would have guessed his side hadn't won.

"The Rangers are always good," Nugget wailed as they piled into the Mustang once again. "But ya'll could beat them if you had a better catcher. Leonard just can't throw anybody out when they steal a base."

Nugget was very observant, and Maggie had to silently agree with her.

R.J. shook his head good-naturedly. "Leonard does the best he can. Besides, we're all here to have fun."

"But don't you like to win?" Maggie asked after he had started the engine.

"Sure," R.J. replied. "But not at the expense of a friend. And if a person can't take losing, he'd better not play at all."

His brown eyes met hers momentarily before he swung the car back onto the street. Maggie had the feeling he wasn't talking about softball. But then what could he have been talking about? Surely not her; he couldn't possibly know that she'd played once and lost, that she had been duped and fooled by a handsome face. Stop it, she scolded herself— your imagination really has gotten out of hand and that was all in the past. Mario was nothing like this man—nothing at all. So why did she shake inside at the mere thought of R.J. kissing her?

It was well after dark when they stopped at a fast food restaurant for supper. Still full of energy, Nugget skipped ahead across the parking lot, while Maggie and R.J. followed at a more sedate pace. As they walked along, his arm settled around the back of her waist with familiar ease. Maggie tried to tell herself she didn't like the warm feeling it created inside her. She tried to tell herself she wouldn't want to be Nugget's mother, or belong to this man for the rest of her life, that she wouldn't want a simple evening like this. Not when she could be dining out on lobster or quail back in New York, a long evening gown and diamonds replacing her jogging shorts.

Maggie glanced over at R.J. as if to assure herself that she really believed what her mind was trying to tell her heart. Yet when he smiled at her, she knew she was failing pitifully. Face it, Maggie, her mind chanted, you're already lost. You were lost yesterday morning when R.J. and Nugget showed up on the doorstep.

"I couldn't possibly eat all this!" Maggie gasped as R.J. placed before her a huge hamburger, French-fried potatoes and a strawberry milkshake.

"Sure you can," he answered easily as he began to eat his own with the relish of a hungry man.

She looked over at Nugget who was happily biting into a foot-long chili dog. The two of them seemed to take eating so lightly, consuming anything they enjoyed and she had to watch everything that went into her mouth.

"I'll look like a blimp by the time I go back to New York," she said in dismay, not making a move to eat.

R.J. looked at her impatiently, almost angrily. "Dammit woman, look at yourself. You're skinny. You need to eat. Forget about modeling for once, and that Phillip or whatever his name is. You're not in New York now, and while you're here you're going to eat and live like a human."

His harsh voice cut her like a knife. She felt hot tears at the back of her eyes, but somehow managed to hold them at bay. No matter what, she couldn't let this man see that he had already gotten under her skin. That would be far more humiliating than anything Mario had ever done to her.

"I said, eat!"

R.J.'s voice broke her trance, and she grabbed the hamburger and bit into it with unladylike movements.

"Maybe Maggie's not hungry," Nugget suggested, hoping to ease the tension that had suddenly sprung up between her father and Maggie.

He looked at Nugget, and continued to speak emphatically. "Oh, she's hungry all right. She's just being ridiculous. I could blow her over with one good breath."

Nugget looked at Maggie with sympathetic eyes, but Maggie didn't notice the child. She was glaring at R.J.'s smug face.

"Would you like to try?" she asked angrily.

His smile was counterfeit. "Maybe I will, just to prove something to you."

Something in his eyes and voice warned Maggie she was stepping into deep water. She looked at him for long moments, then sighed with resignation and reached for the milkshake. It was too painful to argue with him. "If I get too fat to be a model, will you hire me back as a house-keeper?"

At her question, the humor returned to his face and he reached across the tiny table and squeezed her hand, his thumb rubbing lazy little circles on the back of it. The simple touch affected her more than any kiss she'd ever received.

"You wouldn't even need a résumé," he said with a grin, his eyes glinting enigmatically as they met her blue ones.

Maggie ate everything on her plate.

Chapter Seven

In the next two weeks, Maggie learned lots of things, but what struck her the most was that George had been right when he had written to her so long ago. She'd been living, or maybe it had been more like existing, in a vacuum.

Staying with R.J. and Nugget had opened up all kinds of avenues and she woke each morning eagerly anticipating the day ahead. Nugget helped her immensely, and by mid-morning they would usually have the housework finished and plenty of time left on their hands to do as they pleased.

Most days they spent the afternoons in the pool. Maggie was a pretty fair diver, and she worked with Nugget for long hours on the low board. Like R.J., the child was a natural athlete.

Many days they drove to Tony's for fresh milk or bread, or merely as an outing. The fat Mexican would greet Maggie with a laugh and a hug. Maggie had really endeared herself to the man when he found out she could speak fluent Spanish. Now he always conversed with her in his native tongue. Usually he gave Maggie a fatherly kiss on the cheek before they drove away and Nugget teased her unmercifully. The child even told R.J. about it one evening at the dinner table, and he had laughed when Maggie said defensively, "He only does it because I'm George's niece."

"Well, believe me, if I ever kissed you, it wouldn't be for that reason."

His words had caught her off guard, and for a long time after that she couldn't get them out of her head. She still couldn't forget them completely. In the past two weeks, she had grown to know R.J. better than she knew herself, and love for him had blossomed in her heart like the tender petals of a desert flower. The feeling made her doubly aware of him, and she silently hungered for his touch, for some situation to throw them together where he might be tempted to kiss her. So far it hadn't happened, and when he was around she caught herself constantly fantasizing what it would be like to be loved by him.

That was not to say that everything had gone easily. She and R.J. had had several arguments over her cooking and one horribly flaming row over his blue jeans.

A whimsical little smile curved her lips as she recalled the incident. Now, days later, it seemed ridiculous that they could have both been so furious over a minor thing like the laundry. But it had happened and Maggie could still remember the rage on his face when he'd walked into the kitchen and pulled her away from the stove to lead her like a skittish colt toward his bedroom.

"Would you please tell me the meaning of this?" he asked through gritted teeth, flinging open the closet door and pointing to his jeans.

"What do you mean?" she protested. "What's the matter?"

"What's the matter," he mimicked, his sardonic voice setting fire to Maggie's temper. "They're full of wrinkles. They're not ironed, that's what!"

"Ironed!" Maggie gasped. "I've never ironed anything in my life!"

"Then you'd better learn fast because I wouldn't wear these to a dogfight," he assured her in a threatening voice.

"But that's ridiculous! They're only blue jeans," she reasoned. "You work in them; you get them filthy—"

"That's too bad," he shot back. "Just because I'm not one of your executive friends, you think my clothes are unimportant? Well, I wouldn't go out on the job like this for the whole Manhattan bank!" He began ripping the jeans down from the hangers and slinging them across the unmade bed while Maggie stared at him with wild eyes. "Furthermore, I expect every pair to be ironed by tomorrow," he added.

Maggie was outraged and she flounced toward him, her hands on her hips. There was no way she would do it. He was crazy! "Who ironed them before I came?" she demanded.

"I did," he growled.

Maggie smiled sweetly at his answer. "Then you can do it now," she told him and turned to leave.

"No way," he snapped, grabbing her by the shoulder and spinning her around. The force of it caused her hair to spill from its pins, and she glared at him through the tumbling curls. "You'll iron those jeans, or you'll find another contractor."

Maggie's breath drew in sharply. "Then that's exactly what I'll do!" she shouted back and stormed out of his bedroom.

Back in the kitchen, the bacon had burned to a crisp and smoke filled the whole house. She slung the charred meat into the garbage, wishing she could have dumped the whole skillet on his head.

By ten-thirty that morning, Maggie had pulled out the iron and ironing board, but she couldn't make up her mind to use them.

For a long time she sat on a kitchen stool, chin in hand, staring at the offending objects, trying to decide how she could possibly bring herself to give in and iron R.J.'s pants. On the other hand, she realized that R.J. had hired her as his housekeeper and that included doing the laundry. If it was turned around the other way, she would want him to do her house the way she wanted, not just meet her wishes halfway. But her mind battled on, still unable to give in to his ultimatum. The man was so damned domineering at times!

She was still sitting there, thinking over the problem when the telephone rang. It shocked her completely to hear R.J. on the other end.

"Maggie, if you don't really know how to iron, don't worry about it. I'll show you tonight."

Maggie wanted to laugh with relief, and her heart softened as she realized he was really apologizing to her. "I...I think that would be a good idea," she responded, willing at least to meet him halfway, but not willing to admit she'd already gone so far as to pull out the ironing board.

There was a long silence on the line and then he said, "Would you like to go out to dinner tonight?"

Maggie smiled into the telephone, her anger completely forgotten. "I'd love to."

Her mind moving forward to the present, Maggie realized it was stupid of her to become so obsessed with R.J. Especially since he had shown no real signs of interest toward her. Darla Woods had called him twice on the telephone. Hearing parts of the conversation the first time the woman phoned, Maggie could tell that Darla was questioning R.J. about the new arrangements in his household. The next time Darla called she was obviously inviting him out somewhere. Maggie was amazed to find herself sick with relief when he didn't go. Already in her mind she considered him to belong to her. They slept under the same roof, ate at the same table together, watched over the same child. At night he came home to a meal she'd cooked for him. She washed his clothes, made his bed, tidied his house—all the things a woman does for her husband. In her heart it would be traitorous of him to go out with another woman. But her mind kept telling her that that kind of thinking was the height of foolishness. He'd never once even hinted he would like them to be more than friends. He didn't belong to her at all, and if he wanted to go out with a different woman every night, it should mean nothing to her. She was a friend and housekeeper—nothing more.

Even if he did take an interest in her, her mind battled on, theirs was a relationship that could go nowhere. She had a career that she had to go back to, and R. J. Buchanan would never leave the panhandle for anyone or anything. He was a man who seemed to love his freedom, so perhaps that was why he had never touched her more than casually. Maybe that was why she had caught him looking at her with a rather whimsical expression. She didn't know the answers. She only wished that things could be different, so different.

"Maggie, would you like to go down to your house and look it over? It's time we thought about the floor plan or I'll never get it finished this summer."

It was almost dark and Maggie had just finished cleaning the kitchen after their evening meal. They were sitting in the living room. He was seated in one armchair and she was in the other; they had separated the *Dallas Times* and were taking turns with each section.

She lifted her head from the paper to look at him with some surprise. The house had not been mentioned during the past two weeks and, to be honest, she had forgotten it completely. Now that she was staying with R.J. and Nugget, she didn't care if the house ever became habitable. Of course she could never admit this, so she smiled brightly. "Yes, I would. But don't bother if you're too tired. It can wait."

He shook his head and pushed himself up from the half-supine position he usually took in the chair. "No, I don't want it to wait, so go get your shoes on."

She did as he asked, and as they headed toward the open jeep he called to Nugget, who was playing in the backyard.

"Can I bring Walter?" the child called back.

Maggie and R.J. shared an indulgent smiled at this request. "As long as you keep a close watch on him; otherwise, he might never find his way home. And then you'd both be sad."

"I won't let him out of my sight," Nugget promised and raced back to get the horned toad from its wire-mesh house. Maggie had been horrified when she had first seen the girl's pet. A frog with horny spikes sticking out all over was not her idea of a pet at all, much less for a little girl. But Nugget adored the lizardlike animal and had even gotten Maggie around to petting him.

R.J. explained that the horned toad now named Walter was first discovered on the patio one night eating bugs. Obviously Walter liked Nugget, too, because even if he wasn't in his wire house, he wouldn't leave the yard.

"She wants a baby armadillo next." R.J. laughed when Maggie gasped in fright at her first sight of Walter.

"You...you mean one of those squatty little animals that have a shell on the back?"

"Lovely little things, aren't they?" He laughed. " A gift from Mexico. Ugly, but tenacious. You can't help but feel for the creatures."

Maggie shuddered. "I think I'll stick to Gertrude." Gertrude was the mother cat who lived in the barn and produced two healthy litters a year.

Nugget appeared back at the jeep with Walter secure in a shoebox. R.J. helped her into the jeep and then backed out of the drive with a cloud of red dust settling behind them. Maggie had grown used to the dust. She had even grown accustomed to the unceasing wind. It would probably feel strange to step outside and not feel its warm embrace.

The house was just as awful as Maggie remembered. While Nugget played with Walter down by the windmill, she and R.J. walked through the dingy rooms.

"Was there anything in particular you wanted to do with the house?" R.J. asked as he ran a professional eye over the floors and walls. "What kind of floor did you have in mind?"

Maggie looked around her. It was hard to concentrate on the house. She'd rather look at him, and she caught herself doing it more and more these days. He always took his shirt off after supper, and Maggie studied the subtle movements of his muscles flexing as if she had never seen a man's chest before. She didn't know why his brown skin and hard muscles fascinated her so, but they did. Just like the curve of his lip beneath the line of his mustache and the way his tawny eyes flickered when he talked, the way his brows formed a straight line when he was angry. There wasn't anything about the man that didn't charm her, and she had to admit she was helplessly and hopelessly in love with him.

"Maggie, are you listening to me?"

His voice brought her round and she looked at him, a guilty flush on her cheeks. "I... I hadn't really thought about it. Anything that's easy to install. What do you think? Since the house is stucco, a better grade of tile?"

He cast her a wry smile as he kicked one of the loosened squares of tile with the toe of his boot. "I thought you didn't like tile."

"Something like Italian tile, I do. This stuff looks like it belongs on a barber shop floor," she groaned.

R.J. grinned at her. "Well, if that's what you want, it can be easily fixed. Now, about the rooms... Since it's just going to be you using the house, I suggest you do away with this front bedroom completely. I could take out this wall." He hit it with the flat of his hand. "And make an archway. That way you could use it as a large living-room-den combination. The archway would also be in keeping with the southern style.''

"That sounds lovely," Maggie agreed.

They moved to the other rooms and she did her best to concentrate on his words. He seemed to know what she would like before she said anything. They discussed at length the material she would need to buy and the types more suited to her needs.

Several times while R.J. talked, Maggie had the oddest, almost uncontrollable urge to open her mouth and say, There's no need for any of this. I don't want this house. I want to live with you always. I love you—can't you see it?

Of course she didn't say anything of the kind. Instead, she followed him into the kitchen, wiping the sweat from her brow with the back of her hand. Even though the windows were open, the house was uncomfortably hot.

"What kind of cabinets did you want? Pine, ash...?"

Maggie shook her head and lifted the hair from her moist neck with a movement that was unknowingly provocative. "Whatever you suggest. I love the ones in your house, if you could do something like that."

He watched the hair slide back against her neck as she let her arms fall and one side of his mustache lifted in a crooked grin. "Oh, yes, I could do something like that if you want to stay until Christmas. I built those cabinets myself, and with the odd hours I could work on yours, the work would take a while."

Maggie sighed. "Well, that rules out my first choice."

He looked at her with lifted brows. "Why? Can't you stay until then? Can't you afford to?"

Her laugh was bitter as she met his gaze. "Afford to? R.J., I'm sure you know I could afford to buy a dozen houses like this, but that's not it."

She suddenly thought of Phillip chomping at the bit to get her onto another layout, of her father who espoused the adage that being successful at a career was the most important thing in a person's life.

"Then what is it? This Phillip guy who sounds like he tries to own you? Does he have more than business strings on you?"

Maggie's eyes revealed surprise at the question. "No—he would like it to be that way, but I wouldn't."

His eyes narrowed at this answer. "Then what is it? With that kind of money you should be independent, do whatever you want."

She laughed again as she trailed a finger over the steel cabinets, careful to avoid his eyes. She was afraid to look at him too closely, afraid he might see just exactly how she felt about him. "Because I'm a model. That's my job. A person is supposed to take care of her job, isn't she?" She didn't know it, but her lips trembled on the words.

His brown eyes were unexpectedly serious, and he studied her intently until Maggie shifted restlessly against the wall of cabinets, feeling certain he could see inside her.

"Sometimes a person needs to make a change," he answered softly. "How long have you been a model, Maggie?"

"Six years. Since I was eighteen." Astonishingly, the words made her feel old and so alone.

The next instant he was standing close to her, and she could smell the scent that was uniquely his. It clung to his warm skin, and no matter what time of the day she came near him she knew he would have that same male scent that aroused her like some untamed she-cat in the jungle.

"And how long do you intend to go on being a model?"

This time his voice was even softer, and as she met his gaze, one of his hands reached out and touched her hair. She felt his fingers move against it, like the soft flutter of a butterfly.

"I . . . I don't know," she answered quietly, while inside her mind was screaming for him to kiss her, to crush her

ody next to the hard warmth of his until she couldn't even
reathe. "I suppose until my face begins to wrinkle, until
ny body starts losing its shape."

His features grew harsh, and to her utter surprise his
ands closed around the base of her neck. "Your face! Your
ody!" he spat harshly. "What the hell makes you unique?
've dated girls right here in Amarillo that were prettier than
ou, that had figures that would match yours anyday! So tell
ne, Maggie, what is it you've got that other women don't?
Vhy is it that millions want to see you on a magazine cover?
ell me—" he ordered, his fingers now pressing into her
kin.

She was shocked by his words, his attitude and behavior,
nd it was a few moments before the words tumbled from
er lips. "I . . . I don't know—" To her horror, tears began
o spill from her eyes and fall against her cheeks. She never
ried. She was a cool, poised model, an independent
oman.

"Oh, hell, Maggie," he muttered roughly and his fingers
vere suddenly gentle, moving down the slope of her shoul-
ers. They felt like velvet and sandpaper all at the same time
nd Maggie thought how exciting that odd combination was
s it slid over her skin. "I'm sorry—"

"No—" The word burst from her as her fingers lifted to
over his lips. She didn't want to hear apologies or reasons
hy she should stay or leave. She just wanted to touch him,
o kiss his lips, to let the nearness of his body fill her with
nat magic intoxication called love. "Don't say it—just kiss
ne," she whispered.

Her plea was reflected in the drowsy desire in his eyes and
owly, like a film in slow motion, his hands lifted to cup her
ace, then inch by inch his head moved until their lips were
ouching.

Over and over he tasted her lips, like a man exploring
ew, but forbidden territory, until Maggie dissolved in the
ilting flames he was producing inside her.

Her heart was racing at an unbelievable speed, sending th
blood to her head where it drummed a beat of desire in he
ears. Her hands touched his arms, his hair, his shoulders, hi
chest, all the places she had dreamed about touching. Nov
that she was actually doing it, the sensation was like bein
given a sudden dose of a narcotic. She was high on him
high on the love that burned in her heart.

Maggie could not have said how long they stood ther
entwined, their bodies crushed together, their lips meetin
and parting only to meet again, their hands touching an
finding the enticing contours of the other. Maggie only knev
that one minute she was in total bliss, and the next Nug
get's voice could be heard outside the screen door. R.J
twisted away, his breathing ragged as he glanced at Maggi
with condemning eyes.

"We'll be right there, honey," he called to his daughter
and then said to Maggie, "Straighten your clothes and let'
go."

His hard, indifferent voice struck her like a blow, and th
urge to cry was great as she fumbled with the buttons on he
blouse.

"Are you angry at me?" she whispered in confusion.

For a moment she thought his expression was going t
soften, but it didn't, and his eyes were cold, almost blank
as they seemed to look right through her. "No—just mad a
myself."

"But why?" she gasped, not understanding at all how h
could have been kissing her so wantonly one moment an
standing apart from her the next, a cold accusing look on hi
handsome face.

He turned away from her, his fingers running tired]
around the back of his neck. "Let's just say I don't like let
ting myself be used."

The words stabbed her. She couldn't let it stop here
"But...I..." she began, only to have him turn to face he

"I don't want to hear anything. Not anything at all," he interrupted, grabbing her by the arm to lead her toward the back door.

Maggie struggled to compose herself as they left the shelter of the house and met Nugget out in the yard. The child was her bright exuberant self, and Maggie greeted her as normally as she could.

In the jeep on the way home, R.J. ignored both Maggie and Nugget until he heard Nugget ask the question, "Did you show Daddy what you wanted in the house?"

His head twisted to look at the two of them, his lips curling into a derisive sneer. "Yes, she did, Nugget. She showed me exactly what she wanted."

Maggie flinched inwardly at the sardonic inflection in his voice, but Nugget seemed not to notice that anything was amiss.

"But you might forget, Daddy. Did you draw it on paper?" the child insisted.

R.J. snorted as he whipped the jeep into the driveway. "I didn't need to, honey. I've got it memorized completely."

His glance settled on Maggie and her eyes, wounded and pleading, dared to meet his. However, R.J. ignored the pain in her face and turned his complete attention to parking the jeep.

"Nugget, you'd better put Walter back in his house. I think he's had enough excitement for one evening," he told his daughter as the three of them got out of the jeep.

Nugget seemed surprised at her father's request but didn't protest. "Okay." She shrugged, starting toward the backyard with the shoe box in hand. "I don't want him to get sick."

Maggie left the two of them and hurried into the house. She needed to get away from the condemning expression on R.J.'s face. As if she was the one who seduced him! He was the one who had touched her first, she reasoned as she hur-

ried through to her bedroom. *But you were the one wh*
asked him to kiss you, her conscience tacked on.

It was a long time before she heard R.J. and Nugget com
into the house. Maggie stayed in her room and pretended a
interest in a paperback. What else could she do? It was ob
vious R.J. didn't want her company, so how could she g
out and sit with him while Nugget played on the floor with
her dolls?

She tossed the novel to one side and rolled onto her bac
to stare at the ceiling with dry, aching eyes. What had hap
pened? One minute he was kissing her, holding her, and th
next he was a hostile stranger. She would have neve
expected this kind of reaction from him. Not over a fe
kisses. He seemed the kind of man who would probably tak
that sort of thing lightly. But apparently she didn't kno
him, because he hadn't taken it lightly, and the memory o
how he had looked at her caused pain to wind through he
breast. Why? her mind cried. Did he actually find her tha
repulsive?

"Maggie, are you going to read some of my storybook t
me?"

Maggie turned to see that the child was standing by th
bed, her blond hair freshly brushed down over her night
gown. Her little features were sweet, innocent and so like he
father's that it was uncanny. At the sight of her, Maggie fe
a bittersweet ache. At least this child seemed to love an
need her.

"Of course I will," Maggie answered, getting up from th
bed and forcing a bright smile on her face.

"I can't wait to see what happens to Nancy next," Nug
get exclaimed, slipping her hand into Maggie's. "Do yo
think she'll catch the criminals?"

Maggie smiled whimsically at Nugget's doubtful expres
sion. "Well, Nancy Drew is a pretty smart girl. I'll bet she'
figure things out."

Nugget's bedroom was next to R.J.'s, and as they passed it, Maggie noticed he had not yet gone to bed. She didn't know whether to be relieved or not.

With Nugget tucked securely between the sheets Maggie began to read about the teenage sleuth. Nugget was rapt for about five pages, then suddenly she interrupted by asking, "Maggie, are you mad at my daddy?"

Maggie studied the child's worried face and tried to swallow the lump in her throat. "No, of course not," she answered. "Why should I be?"

Nugget's face was a study of confusion. "Well, you and Daddy always sit and talk to each other at night, but tonight you stayed in your room."

How perceptive children were, Maggie thought. "That's just because I was tired tonight. I wanted to rest."

Nugget's brown eyes lit up hopefully. "Then you're not mad? You're not going back to New York?"

Maggie shook her head, wondering with a sinking heart if that was what R.J. was wishing she would do. If she left now, it would hurt Nugget. But that was nothing to what it would do to Maggie; it would simply shatter her.

"No, not now. But remember I do have to go back when summer is over," she reminded the child.

"Nugget, I think it's time you were asleep."

Both females looked up to see R.J. standing in the doorway, one shoulder propped against the doorframe. Maggie's eyes met his only briefly before she leaned down to kiss Nugget's cheek.

"Good night, pumpkin. See you in the morning."

She slipped out of the room just as R.J. was bending to kiss the same cheek, and Maggie's eyes were wet by the time she had made it outside to the patio.

Warmth and quiet enveloped her as she lay back on the lounge to study the stars. The sky was enormous out here in Texas. It appeared to go on forever, just like the flat rolling prairie around them. At first she had thought this a godforsaken place, but now she knew it was really a place with soul, a rough place that inched its way into your heart before you were ever aware of it.

She was unaware of R.J.'s footsteps on the patio until he took the chair next to hers. More than surprised by his appearance, Maggie said nothing to acknowledge him, and for long minutes they sat there in silence. She wanted to say so much to him but was afraid to speak a word in case it might suddenly make him vanish.

"You must like it out here," he said finally. "You're out here every night."

There was no anger or derision in his voice, and Maggie warmed to the friendlier tone.

"Yes," she acknowledged. "Living in an apartment in New York, I have no place to do this. And even if there was, it wouldn't be the same, or even safe."

R.J. grunted in disgust, and Maggie just had to turn to look at him. It seemed that was the only thing her eyes would do.

"Must be a helluva life."

Maggie sighed and shifted on the lounge. "I'd never thought of it before, but I think of it often now."

He didn't say anything, and the silence stretched once again. Maggie wondered if he was thinking about what it had been like to kiss her. Was the thought burning in his mind as it was in hers, or was he already trying to put the incident out of his head?

Without any warning, he was suddenly squatted on his heels close beside her, and Maggie's eyes widened in surprise as his hand curved around her fingers.

"Maggie—I'm sorry about this evening. I shouldn't have been so harsh with you, especially when it was probably more my fault than yours."

The pain in her chest made it difficult to breathe, and she took a deep breath as she met his eyes through the dark.

ness. "Fault? You make it sound like we committed a crime," she replied bitterly.

"It would be a crime for me to become involved with you. I don't want to do that, Maggie Winslow."

"Why?" she whispered, unable to tear her eyes from his.

His free hand lifted and Maggie withered with longing as the back of it brushed lightly against her cheek.

"If you want me to tell you simply, you're too rich for my blood—in more ways than one."

"You're being presumptuous, Mr. Buchanan, if you think I want to become involved with you." Her voice was deliberately cool. He was hurting her and it wasn't in her nature to remain passive, to take it without some kind of retaliation. If she could somehow prick his male ego, then that would be some kind of small compensation at least.

Her words had some effect on him because his hands were suddenly on her shoulders. "Then what was all that?" he demanded. "Just a come-on, a tease act? Do you get a thrill out of using your beauty to turn men on?"

His words infuriated her. She tried to control her rising temper. "If you think I'm promiscuous, you couldn't be more wrong."

His smile was mocking. "You don't expect me to believe you haven't slept with a man before. The idea is ridiculous!"

Maggie twisted from his grasp, her breathing rapid and shallow. "No more ridiculous than you thinking I was trying to entice you to my bed just because I asked you to kiss me," she hissed.

It was incredibly quiet when the sound of her voice died away. She was trembling all over, and her mind held flashes of packing her suitcases, of the long drive back to New York, and facing Phillip and his pious selfishness.

"Then why did you want to kiss me?" he questioned softly.

The unexpected tenderness in his voice was Maggie's un-
doing, and for the second time that evening warm tears
trickled down her cheeks. Impatiently, she wiped them away
with the back of her hand, hating herself for being so weak
and emotional. How could she say because I love you? She
couldn't. Not when he had just made it clear he didn't want
to be involved with her. If she confided her feelings now it
would only complicate things further.

"I don't know," she stammered, unable to look at him.
"I just wanted to be close to you."

To her surprise, he chuckled as he shook his head in
disbelief. "Maggie, Maggie, I have to believe you now. Only
an innocent could say something like that. Don't you know
that you can't be that close to a man without his thoughts
going to the main event?"

Maggie's body grew hot at the picture he was producing.
"You didn't like kissing me?" she asked bleakly.

"For God's sake, Maggie," he groaned impatiently.
"That's what I've been trying to tell you. I liked it too
damned much."

Maggie whirled around to face him, her hands closing
over his strong forearms, her eyes pleading. "Then why are
we quarreling? Why aren't we kissing instead?"

He shook his head. "Because I'm the way I am and
you're the way you are, and when you go back to New York
I don't want bitter, angry, feelings between us. I want us to
remember each other as friends instead of as regrets we'd
rather not recall."

"Do you want me to leave?" The question scared her to
death but it had to be asked.

His sigh was heavy, his expression revealing fatigue. "No,
I don't want you to go. And Nugget already loves you. It
would break her heart if you left before the summer was
over."

Maggie's hands slid down his arms and curved around his
tough fingers. "Then what are we supposed to do?" she

asked bitterly. "Am I supposed to look at you and say I can't touch you because you're from Texas, because you wear jeans and boots, because you drive a jeep and drink beer out of the can? Are you going to look at me and say I daren't touch her because she's from New York, because she's a famous model, because she wears silk and diamonds and goes to Broadway and the Caribbean for entertainment?"

He didn't look at her as he answered but gazed instead at the horses nipping the tough, sparse grass that grew around the edges of the fence post. "Since you put it that way, yes, that's exactly what we're going to do."

His voice was flat, and Maggie wished she could be as unfeeling as he seemed to be. But then, he didn't love her; she didn't produce in him that euphoric state that causes a person to lose all rational thought.

"And that won't be hard for you?" she asked in a defeated voice.

He suddenly pulled her to her feet. "I've done harder things in my time," he answered. "Now come on—let's go in and have a beer together."

Maggie followed him into the house, her mind whirling with his words. It might be easy for him, but to leave here was going to be the hardest thing she'd ever done in her life.

Chapter Eight

Helen Mangrum was a woman in her late fifties with beautiful silver hair that she wore in a pageboy style more fitting to a younger person. Yet it suited her perfectly, for she was extremely youthful looking with her trim figure and beautifully tanned skin. She was open and amusing and pleasant to be around. Maggie had met her more than a week ago and already she valued the older woman's friendship. Her husband, Jim, worked for R.J. as a carpenter. Helen told Maggie that some years back Jim had owned a very successful construction company. His success showed in their style of living—they had a huge, luxurious house, a kidney-shaped pool and a four-car garage. However, it was obvious they weren't money-oriented people because Helen and Jim had both been in agreement to sell the company, opting for Jim to work for someone else and thus take the strain of running the business off his shoulders. Apparently, the move from Dallas had been the right one, because the couple seemed extremely happy now that they had time to enjoy their lives with each other.

One day the previous week Helen had called and introduced herself, and had begged Maggie and Nugget to drive over for lunch. It had been a delightful outing. Maggie hadn't realized how much she had missed conversation with another woman until she'd driven home later that afternoon.

Now, sitting in Helen's bright kitchen once again, she fiddled with the spoon in her iced tea, stirring it for the hundredth time as Helen talked of her upcoming anniversary party. But this time conversation was the last thing on Maggie's mind.

"I really think buffet would be much better than sit-down, don't you?" Helen's warm drawl traveled over to Maggie as the other woman rinsed salad greens under the tap.

"It is much easier," Maggie replied absently.

"And it would work perfectly out by the pool," Helen went on cheerily. "That way we could dance, too. Jim loves to dance, so I've already planned to hire a small band." Her voice stopped and then she asked, "Maggie, are you listening, or am I boring you with all this?"

Dropping the greens into the sink, Helen walked over to where Maggie sat perched on a bar stool, her long tanned legs crossed, her chin in her palm.

Maggie shook her head, a guilty little flush across her cheeks. "Of course you're not boring me. I . . . I'm just not with it today."

Helen's hazel eyes studied Maggie a bit more closely. "Oh, bad night?"

Maggie sighed as she pushed the heavy blond curls away from her face. Bad, she thought wryly—*bad* wasn't the word for it—more like tormented. She had sat out on the patio and watched R.J. drive away with Darla Woods for the third time in the past week. It had been almost more than she could bear, seeing the two of them together, knowing he would probably touch her, kiss her, possibly even make love to her. She wanted to scream at him. She wanted to say she should be the one by his side, the one he should be smiling at, the one he should be making love to. But of course she couldn't do that. Instead she had made polite conversation with Darla and wished them a pleasant evening as the two of them had driven away in R.J.'s Mustang. The sight had torn jagged cracks in her heart that were never likely to heal.

Nugget had not been as polite as Maggie. Since her father had shown a renewed interest in Darla, the child had been petulant and sulky. On the nights her father brought Darla to the house preceding a date, Nugget stayed in her room. She made her dislike of the woman obvious, big tears rolling down her face as she told her daddy that she and Maggie needed his company more than Darla Woods did.

Maggie had been unable to stand that particular scene, because Nugget was saying exactly what was in her own heart, and she had walked away, the sound of R.J.'s voice as he tried to placate his daughter barely edging into her consciousness. She could think of nothing but his hands, his lips, his face and body. They belonged to her. Her heart told her so, and she could not accept sharing him with another woman. Since the night they had kissed in the hot, dusty house, she had become like a woman possessed. He was in her heart, her very soul, and she didn't know which way to turn to drive him out.

"R.J. was out and I didn't sleep soundly until he returned," Maggie reasoned carefully. At least half the statement was true.

"Oh? Working overtime? That's unusual for R.J."

Maggie smiled wryly. "You could call it that if you describe Darla Woods as work."

Helen threw up her hands in exasperation at the woman's name and walked back to the sink with a shake of her head. "Oh, that woman! I can't see what a charming man like R.J. could possibly see in her. I've never been able to figure it out."

"Probably just looking at her would be enough for most men," Maggie replied, careful to keep any sting from her voice. Even though she liked Helen very much, she wasn't quite ready to confide her love for R.J. to anyone. It would be senseless, anyway.

"Yes, but R.J. is not just any man. He's a man who would want and need more than a face and figure, and believe me, that's all Darla Woods will ever be. Her idea of life is money, money and money. All in that order."

"Obviously R.J. doesn't think so. Or maybe she shows him a different side," Maggie replied. There had to be some explanation, but Maggie wasn't sure she wanted to know it. Just linking their two names together made her sick inside.

Helen began tearing the greens into a large salad bowl. "You could be right. I think Darla takes an entirely different pose around R.J."

Maggie left the bar stool and went to stand beside Helen to watch the woman snip green onion into the bowl. "Er, how long has R.J. dated Darla, anyway?"

"Mm, well, let's see.... Probably about a year now, if I recall it right. They met when R.J. was doing her father's new clinic. He's a doctor, you see," she explained.

"They must have plenty of money," Maggie mused out loud.

"Yes, they do. From what I gather, Darla gets what Darla wants."

"Then it must not be money she looks for in R.J."

Helen laughed at this, her hips swinging gently as she walked over to place the salad in the middle of the table. "I'm sure you know by now that if a woman looks at R.J. she doesn't see money."

Maggie blushed, thinking back to her first thoughts when she had seen the man. "No, I guess not."

"Don't get me wrong—R.J. has plenty of money. He's made it all by himself, too. No handouts from his parents. Which is really incredible at his age. I asked him once how he'd done it. He said he'd found a banker willing to trust him and then he'd put his talent to work to make sure the banker had never lost faith in him. Simple for R.J., I suppose. It sure wasn't that easy for Jim. But back to the other thing—when a woman first looks at R.J., she doesn't think about his intelligence or money. Not with sex and charm written all over him."

Needing to keep busy, Maggie began placing napkins and silverware on the quilted place mats. "He doesn't live like he has money or is a successful businessman. I mean, not like most people would."

Helen chuckled as her fingers deftly arranged cheese and crackers on a silver tray. "No, but R.J.'s a bit of an outlaw. I suppose that's why I love him so. You know the old adage that ladies love outlaws. But I think Darla believes she can change all of that once she has him hooked. You know, the dinner jacket bit, two-story house and golf on Sunday."

A sense of revulsion gripped Maggie's stomach. That anyone would want to change R.J. was incomprehensible. She loved him just as he was. Never would she want him to change. But if he and Darla should marry... Would he be that gullible? Did he love the woman that much?

"Do you think they might actually marry?" Maggie hoped the panic couldn't be heard in her voice as she squeaked out the question.

Helen shrugged. "Who's to say? To tell you the truth, I think R.J. enjoys being single too much. And Darla's had a whole year. I think for R.J. to marry, it's going to have to be someone very special."

"I hope so," she breathed out a sigh, then hastily tacked on, "for Nugget's sake. Darla would make a horrid stepmother."

Helen looked up from the table, her green eyes twinkling. "What about you, Maggie? Are you interested in marriage? I can vouch for it. It's wonderful."

Maggie laughed to hide her discomfiture. "Oh, no, not me. Once bitten, twice shy."

"Maggie—" Helen chuckled knowingly "—we've all been bitten. But when you find the right man, you won't be shy."

No, she hadn't been shy at all, she thought, recalling how shamelessly she had asked R.J. to kiss her. But then Helen couldn't know that Maggie had fallen in love with a man who would never return her love.

"I'll try to remember that." Maggie smiled, but there was a cold ache around her heart.

"Why don't you go call Nugget? I believe lunch is ready."

Maggie started toward the sliding glass doors, glad for a reason to end the conversation about R.J. and marriage. In her mind, the two could mean nothing but heartache.

For an hour after lunch, the two women discussed the party, then took a leisurely swim in the crystal blue swimming pool. All in all, it was an enjoyable afternoon. Nugget, too, seemed in better spirits after showing Helen how well she had learned to dive. Maggie was glad. The child had been rather dispirited since R.J. had been seeing so much of Darla. Maggie could easily understand this; her own spirits had hit rock bottom.

Maggie was doing the supper dishes when R.J. and Nugget came in from feeding the horses. The past few days Maggie hadn't joined them in the daily chore. Since the night he'd said he didn't want an involvement with her, Maggie had made sure she didn't push her presence on him. If she was asked along on an outing, then she went; otherwise, she stayed by herself, filling her time with little chores in the house or reading a book out on the patio. It was better that way, she told herself; she wouldn't be tempted to make a fool of herself twice.

"Maggie, how would you like a different job?"

R.J.'s words caused her to freeze and her hands stopped moving in the soapy water, unable to push the sponge across the dirty plate. "What . . . what do you mean?"

"My secretary is going on vacation for a week. I thought you might be willing to take her place."

As she heard him walking up beside her, she let out a pent-up breath and began to scrub the ironstone plate. She was so relieved he wasn't asking her to leave that she could actually smile as he leaned lazily against the cabinet counter.

"What about Nugget? What would we do with her?"

"We'll take her with us," he answered easily. "She's stayed with me at the office many times before. She has her own little desk and usually doesn't get in the way. So that will pose no problem."

Maggie's brows lifted with interest. "What would I be doing?"

"Answering the telephone. Filing. Just simple things. But if you think it and the housekeeping would be too much to handle, then I could get Darla."

Maggie bristled at the mention of the woman's name. "In other words, you think Darla is capable of working at the office, then going home to do the cooking and cleaning," she said tartly.

R.J.'s laugh was like the crow of a rooster. "Darla doing housework!" he roared, letting out another boom of laughter.

Maggie flung the wet sponge down on the countertop. "And is that so funny?" she gritted. "I do it, don't I?" Did he think Darla Woods was that much better than she was? The thought infuriated Maggie.

All at once he was near her, his fingers under her chin, his expression serious. "Yes, you do. Devoutly, I'd say."

As his thumb moved across her chin, Maggie quivered in response. She wanted to move the step or two that sepa-

ated them, to lay her cheek against his hard chest, to hear
he strong beat of his heart. She shook her head to dispel the
rge. "Is something wrong with that?"

"Not at all. I find it a most admirable trait," he an-
wered softly. "Now, do you want the job or not?"

"I get the feeling that you're trying to charm me into
his."

With a laugh, he dropped his hand from her chin and
hook his head at her in a disbelieving manner. "Give me
ome credit, Maggie, for thinking you're more than just a
it of blond fluff that can be easily manipulated. If that was
he case, I would hardly want you looking out for my busi-
ess."

"But you could get Darla," she stated, wondering why he
asn't asking the other woman instead of her.

"Yeah, I could. But I happen to think things will run
moother if you're there."

She brightened, but tried not to show it. "Why?"

He shrugged. "Just my personal opinion."

"Okay, I'll do it," she said, contented enough with his
eason. "I've got a degree in business management. This
ill be my first chance to use it."

Maggie could feel his curious eyes upon her and knew that
he had surprised him.

"You never mentioned that. When did you have time to
o to college? I thought modeling took all your time."

"I took night classes whenever my schedule would al-
ow."

"You must have been very determined."

Maggie nodded, then returned her attention to the sink-
ul of dirty dishes. "I was, but I knew I couldn't be a model
or the rest of my life."

"You've already made enough money for the rest of your
fe. What is it with you? Do you have an incessant need for
oney or work?"

"Neither. I just can't see myself retiring at thirty-five, jus
sitting around growing useless and lazy. I don't believe i
that. Business management is something that could take m
in an infinite number of directions."

"What about marriage?"

The question jolted her, and for a moment she closed he
eyes, trying to force away the images in front of them. I
would be masochistic to think of R.J. and herself linked i
that spiritual and physical union. She had to stop thinkin
that way before it got entirely out of hand. "If I found th
right man. So far the ones I've known have been selfish an
unpredictable."

"Maybe you expect too much from them," he sug
gested.

"Maybe so," she replied stoically, while inside hysterica
laughter bubbled up in her throat. Standing right here be
side her was the man who met all her expectations except th
one she needed most—love for her.

Maggie was in for one of the greatest shocks of her life th
following Monday when she went to work with R.J. Sh
expected him to have a thriving but modest business, mor
than likely working out of one of those portable meta
buildings. How wrong she had been!

Buchanan Construction Company was a huge enter
prise, covering at least three acres. The offices were in
modern brick building with lots of plate glass. She late
learned that R.J. had designed and built it himself. On th
remainder of the lot, there were rows of storage barn
housing all sorts of building materials. There was also a
endless amount of heavy equipment and several men on for
lifts moving sacks of cement and lumber across the wor
yard.

Maggie had been flabbergasted, yet had kept her sur
prise to herself. Obviously R.J. was rich and a very talente
engineer. He had a number of people employed for him, an

he also learned that not only had he constructed important buildings in Amarillo, but he had also built them in El Paso, Albuquerque and Santa Fe.

It was so hard to connect R.J., the easy-living R.J., who loved to play softball, who drove her and Nugget around in his Mustang and bought them ice cream cones for a night on the town, with the successful businessman.

Acting as R.J.'s secretary was a very satisfying and interesting job. The business of construction had many different facets to it, and R.J. knew each one so well. His success came as no surprise. His diplomatic charm didn't hurt things, either.

Blueprints, drafts, closed bids, purchase orders and many more elements were a part of R.J.'s day, and even without her emotional involvement with him, she would have found the business very intriguing. It was satisfying to know that in some small part she was helping construct a beautiful building, a place that would harbor many lives, see many things happen within its walls. It was a far cry from creating an illusion before a camera lens.

Thursday turned out to be a terribly busy day. The telephone rang off the hook and several potential clients, including one city official, came in for meetings all before lunch.

Maggie finally found a free moment to speak to R.J. just before noon when he was preparing to leave for a building site.

She stuck one last file into the steel cabinet and hurried over to him as he reached for his hard hat and started toward the door.

"Do you need the jeep?" she asked.

He turned to look at her. "Not if you do. I'll drive a company truck."

She was surprised to find how nervous she was. "Well, Nugget and I planned to visit the hairdresser on my lunch hour."

"Fine," he agreed. "If you're not back by one-thirty, I'
have Roger watch the office for you."

Roger was a young man in his late twenties who worke
at everything from sawing and hammering to negotiatin
new contracts. He was witty and good-looking in a tanned
blond way, and Maggie had become friends with him righ
from the start.

"Thank you. I appreciate it."

"By the way," he said, "don't bother with supper thi
evening. Darla and I are going out."

Maggie's fingers clenched at this announcement. "That'
work out fine because Nugget and I are going shopping to
night, then later meeting Roger for dinner."

R.J.'s brows lifted to a sardonic line. "That's rather fast
isn't it?"

"Not really. Roger's an easy person to know. And afte
all, I'm sure if you trust him with your business, then you'r
sure to trust him with your housekeeper."

"The two are hardly the same," he said, frowning.

Maggie opened her mouth to retort, but just then Nugge
appeared behind her.

"Can I wear my miniskirt tonight, Maggie? I promise I'
sit like a proper lady."

Maggie ruffled the child's hair. They had grown so clos
in the past weeks that inside Maggie actually felt like Nug
get's mother. "Of course, sweetheart."

Nugget beamed, then her eyes suddenly darkened as sh
looked at her father. "We're gonna have much more fu
than you and Darla, too. We won't have to go to some stuff
restaurant that brings you one thing at a time, like Darl
wants."

"I hope you have a whale of a time, Nugget," he told her

From the look on his face, Maggie doubted the word
were sincere and she wondered why. It shouldn't matter t
him whether she and Nugget chose an evening out wit
Roger over an evening at home alone.

Maggie knew nothing of the hairstylists in that part of the country, but she had already decided to take her chances and here was no backing out now. Besides, she told herself, she was sick of having to wear her hair twisted up to stay cool. She had been wanting a new style for a while, and this summer was the best time to get one. The fact that R.J. had suggested it was merely a coincidence, or so she kept reminding herself.

Now she was standing in the foyer of an expensive-looking salon with Nugget's little hand clinging to hers.

"This place looks good enough for a queen," Nugget whispered. "Are you sure we're at the right one?"

Maggie smiled down at the awed child. "Yes, I'm sure. Now be a good girl. Here comes the lady to take us back."

The attendant was an older woman dressed in a subdued but expensive gray dress. Maggie gave her their names and the austere lady led them to a larger room that displayed a row of pink dryers and shampoo bowls.

Maggie instructed Nugget's stylist as to what she would like to have done with the child's hair, then put herself into the hands of a man named Fred with blazing red hair that pushed wildly about his head. He was fortyish with a paunchy stomach and once he started talking, Maggie felt completely at east with him.

"I feel sure I should know you," he said after a few minutes. He was studying her image in the mirror after giving her a relaxing shampoo. Her hair hung in sleek wet curls around her face and shoulders. "Have you been in the salon before?"

Maggie shook her head, a secretive little smile on her lips. "No, you've probably seen me on a magazine cover," she hinted broadly.

His russet-colored eyebrows lifted, then recognition streaked across his face. "My God, you're Maggie!"

Maggie smiled, accustomed to this type of reaction. "Yes."

His hands lifted her hair to let it fall almost reverently down her back. "And you're going to let *me* do your hair?"

"Yes, I am," she answered confidently. It was foolish to think André was the only one who should style her hair.

"But... doesn't that—"

"Famous Frenchman do my hair," she finished for him. "Yes, André Bonet is my beauty consultant. But he's not in Amarillo, Texas. Since you are here, I'm sure you'll do just as good a job. Besides, I want something different. I want you to create a new style for me, something chic, but something you might find on a hundred different women in Amarillo."

Fred went red in the face. "Cut! It would be a sacrilege. And for me to do it ... I—"

Maggie folded her arms determinedly beneath the pink plastic cape. "I won't be dissuaded."

Fred rolled his eyes in resignation, and realizing what a trying task she'd burdened him with, she laid her hand on his arm. "Don't worry, Fred. I just want to be treated like any other lady who walks in here."

Fred nodded with a grateful smile and proceeded to section her hair into four large areas. He worked with swift, deft movements, and after several minutes had passed he began to loosen up and gain more confidence.

"Are you here in Amarillo on business?" he asked. "I haven't read it in the papers."

"No. I'm vacationing."

His brows lifted as if to ask why a famous model would choose to vacation on the plains of Texas. "I'm staying with a friend of my deceased uncle. He owns a construction company here in Amarillo," she explained.

"He?" Fred asked slyly. "Are you talking about Richard Buchanan?"

Maggie felt heat spreading across her cheeks. "Why, yes, do you know him?"

Fred nodded. "I know of him, but then most everyone round the city knows of him. He's making quite a name for imself. Were you here at the big celebration for the opening of the new doctors' clinic he constructed?"

Maggie shook her head. He must mean the one connected with Darla Woods's father. Jealousy stabbed through her at the thought.

"It's quite a building," Fred went on. "I think one of the most beautiful here in the city. I saw Mr. Buchanan's picture in the papers when he built a new art museum in Santa Fe. Quite a handsome guy, and so young to be so successful." He shrugged and laughed good-naturedly. "Ah, but some men have it all."

"Yes, he's very talented," Maggie agreed, silently glad Fred wasn't a gossip columnist. What a field day they would have if they knew she were living in the same house with a man like R.J.

When Maggie's hair was finally dry, she shook her head and laughed as the blond waves fell back into place. Fred had cut it to curl inward at midneck, leaving the top long enough to fall to one side in a sleek wave over her right eye. The remainder dipped and waved as it pleased, giving her an elegant, but still casual style.

"Oh, Fred, I love it. I feel like a new woman. I look so different and my head feels light and free!" Maggie exclaimed.

"It should," Fred said, a pleased expression on his face. "You've probably lost two pounds of hair. And I think I must agree with you. I like this new you. Your old style spoke obvious glamour. But this look is fresh and innocent, yet still adds a trace of mystery to those incredible eyes of yours."

"It's marvelous," Maggie cried ecstatically. "And believe me, Fred, there are plenty of models I know who would think nothing of flying out here to get you to do their hair, once I tell them what a great job you do."

Fred was obviously flabbergasted by the compliment. "I
don't know what to say—it's been like a dream come true.
Imagine! Fred Euell creating a new style for the great Maggie!"

They talked on for a few minutes as Fred told her how to
take care of her new style until Nugget interrupted them with
her arrival. The child's eyes grew enormous as she saw
Maggie's short hair.

"How do you like it?" Maggie asked, laughing as she ran
her fingers through the soft waves.

"It's sooo pretty!" Nugget exclaimed. "Daddy won't be
able to quit looking at you."

Fred's eyebrows peaked with interest at the child's statement, and Maggie laughed in embarrassment. "Nugget,
you're the one who will hold your daddy's interest. You
look like a princess."

Nugget's hair had been French braided, then twisted into
a chignon. It showed off the innocent line of her little face
and enhanced the brightness of the brown eyes that were
glowing with joy.

While Fred chatted with Nugget, Maggie discreetly tucked
an outrageous tip beneath his hand mirror. The money was
nothing to Maggie, and she wanted this man to know how
greatly she appreciated his efforts.

"Goodbye, Maggie." He smiled as she and Nugget started
to depart. "It's been such a pleasure. And let me say that
you're a hundred times more lovely than your photographs."

"Thank you, Fred. Perhaps I'll see you again before I
leave Amarillo."

"I'd be delighted." He smiled again and gallantly kissed
her cheek.

"Wow! That man really liked you!" Nugget exclaimed as
they walked across the parking lot to R.J.'s jeep.

"That's because I'm a well-known model," Maggie said

"I don't think so," Nugget reasoned as the two of them climbed into the jeep. "I think it's because you're so pretty and nice."

"Thanks, moppet." Maggie smiled, touching the little girl's freckled nose. "You're sweet, but you've got a lot to learn."

As they drove through the city streets back to R.J.'s office building, Maggie thought how ridiculous she must look wearing a skirt and heels while driving a dusty, dented army jeep. A month ago, she wouldn't have been caught in such a position, but now it was rather amusing, and even natural to be grinding the gears and ignoring the whistles of the male passersby.

"I'm back," Maggie announced as she stuck her head around the door of the warehouse. Roger was working on a set of cabinets, and he looked up at the sound of her voice.

"Hey, you look scrumptious!" He grinned as he took in the drastic change of hairstyle. "Did I say eight-thirty? Well, let's make it seven."

Maggie laughed. "Whatever you say. See you later."

"Remember, the fountain in the mall," he reminded her.

Maggie answered with a wave, then turned to walk down the long corridor that led back to the office. As she did, she collided into a rock wall of a chest and looked up to see the harsh lines of R.J.'s face.

"Er, I'm sorry. I didn't see you," she hastily apologized.

"How could you—you weren't looking," he said sharply, then added dryly, "I thought you were here to answer the phone?"

"Oh?" Maggie questioned in mock innocence. "Is it ringing?"

"How should I know," he snarled.

Maggie made an effort to pull away from the hands that had closed around her upper arms when she had walked into him. "Then why don't you let me go see," she told him in a

voice that matched his. "It might be the president wanting
you to renovate part of the White House."

With a dark scowl on his face, he loosened his grip and
she started to march past him. Before she slipped away, he
pulled her back roughly.

"Just a minute. What have you done to your hair?"

As his eyes roamed over her, she unconsciously lifted a
hand to the thick mass of blond waves. "Just gotten rid of
a major part of it," she answered.

His scowl suddenly deepened. "I hope you didn't do this
just because I suggested it," he said.

"How conceited," Maggie snapped. Never in a million
years would she want this man to guess she might have any
kind of feelings for him. Especially not when he seemed to
enjoy flaunting Darla in front of her face. "I'm not Darla,"
she reminded him.

His brown eyes darkened as his hands closed around her
upper arms. "No, you're not," he said a bit too smoothly.
"So maybe I shouldn't treat you like her."

"What do you mean?" she asked, her breath coming in
short angry spurts as she made an effort to free herself from
his grasp.

"You know what I mean," he muttered, then pulled her
into his arms and hungrily fastened his mouth over hers.

Maggie was too shocked to struggle, and by the time she
thought about it, her senses had already turned traitor. Her
fingers gripped the sides of his waist, her mouth yielded to
part beneath the hard warmth of his. He had vowed not to
touch her again, but he was—and Maggie had neither the
strength nor the desire to fight him or her own turbulent
emotions.

"See, Maggie. I told you Daddy would like your hair,"
Nugget sang out from the other end of the hallway.

R.J. instantly stepped away from Maggie, his face filled
with regret as he looked at the flush on her cheeks, the slight

quiver of her hand as she tucked a strand of hair behind her ear.

However, Maggie didn't see this emotion on his face. She couldn't bring herself to look at him. Instead, her eyes focused on the child at the end of the hallway. Obviously it delighted the child to see her daddy kissing Maggie. This was progress in the right direction, as far as she was concerned. Maggie's heart contracted painfully at the thought. The poor child didn't understand her father had only been kissing her out of anger and spite.

"Don't you think Maggie's hair is beautiful, Daddy?"

R.J.'s brown eyes passed over Maggie slowly. Their amber gaze hardly even glanced at her hair, but more or less caressed the soft line of her lips. "Yes, very nice," he said in a distracted tone.

"Fred thought so, too. He kissed Maggie's cheek when we left the salon." Nugget sighed and twirled around on one toe. "I hope I'm beautiful like Maggie when I grow up. Then all the men will want to kiss me, too."

"I don't think you need to worry about kissing right now, Nugget," R.J. groaned, then began to propel his daughter down the hallway.

Maggie stared after them, a terrible ache in her chest. It was a long time before she was composed enough to go back into his office.

Maggie was grateful for the evening out with Nugget and Roger. She didn't want to have any time on her hands to think about R.J. and Darla. Most of all, she didn't want to relive those moments in the hall when he'd kissed her so savagely.

Nugget was an obedient child, and she loved getting new clothes. Maggie thoroughly enjoyed splurging on the girl, justifying her generosity by saying school was just ahead and she would be needing lots of new clothes.

Maggie wasn't sure what Nugget enjoyed the most—picking out clothes for Maggie, or for herself. But as for Maggie, she purchased clothes for herself almost recklessly, buying most anything that looked stylish and caught her eye. She had gained weight. Not just a pound or two, but fifteen pounds! None of her own clothes fitted and she knew Phillip would be horrified to know she was wearing two sizes larger. He would also be horrified to know she was buying clothes from a chain store, instead of having them tailored exclusively. But that was too bad, Maggie mused. So what if another woman had a dress of violet poplin buttoned down the front, or a pair of black jeans with a tiny white stripe running through them. She didn't want to be unique anymore. She just wanted to be herself, and if Phillip didn't like her that way she didn't really care. She only wished she felt that way toward R.J.

Maggie and Nugget met Roger at the fountain, as planned, and walked through the busy shopping mall to a family restaurant. The meal was excellent and since Roger was young and still a bachelor, the innocence of Nugget's childish remarks kept him laughing. After the meal, they ambled back through the mall to window-shop at the endless array of shops. Nugget somehow managed to persuade them to enter a pet shop where Maggie found herself looking at everything from kittens to huge gray rats to colorful macaws.

Nugget was still chattering about it when they arrived back home. However, she became quiet suddenly, as did Maggie, when they walked into the living room, their arms loaded with packages, and found R.J. sitting there drinking a beer. They had both expected him to be out late with Darla.

Once the initial surprise was over, Nugget ran to hop in her daddy's lap and kiss his cheek. "We had such fun, Daddy," she eagerly told him. "Maggie bought me bunches of clothes and we ate lasagna then we went in a pet shop that had the most beautiful birds. My favorite was the cockatoo. Do you think we might get one for a pet?''

He studied his daughter's face. ''What about the armadillo?''

She gave him a reflection of one of his own beguiling smiles. ''Well, the bird would be in the house and the armadillo would be outside,'' she reasoned.

He grunted with amusement. ''I'll think about it,'' he promised, patting his daughter's cheek.

Maggie noticed the humor had left his face when he turned to her. ''Did you use my charge card, like I told you?''

Maggie chose not to look at him as she began drawing some of their things out of paper sacks and boxes. ''Not this time. I wanted to buy Nugget some things on my own before I go back home to New York.''

''Another one of your ploys, Maggie?''

The clipped tone of his voice and the suggestive question prompted her to look at him. ''Ploys? I don't know what you're talking about.'' It was the truth. But then she had to admit that these days she hardly ever knew what he was really thinking or feeling.

He ignored her reply and asked, ''Did Roger pick out that outfit you have on?''

His question surprised her, and she found herself looking down at the deep turquoise pant suit. It was crisp cotton fashioned into tight capri-style pants and a sleeveless overblouse that slashed at the neckline. She had cinched it tightly at her waist with a white leather belt to match her white high-heeled sandals. The outfit was definitely Marilyn Monroe, and because the weight she had gained had filled out her curves, the style was perfect for her. It made her feel young and glamorous, especially with her shorter hair brushing sensuously against the curve of her neck.

''No,'' she answered. ''I barely know the man.''

"Then why did you go out with him?" His eyes seemed riveted to her body as if he was just now seeing the full curves emphasized by her clothes.

Maggie shrugged and pretended an interest in the peach-colored dress in her hands. "My word, R.J., we only had dinner together, with a child along at that. I hardly call that going out, do you?" Besides, she thought churlishly, it's none of your business.

He didn't answer, and when Maggie decided he wasn't going to, she turned to look at him. By now Nugget had climbed off his lap and was absorbed in trying on a new pair of sandals. R.J. was staring out at the darkening night as he lifted the beer can to his lips. He looked so aloof and unapproachable that Maggie scooped up her things and said, "Come on, Nugget. It's time you were in bed, especially if you want to hear another chapter of Nancy Drew."

Much later, after several pages of the detective story, Maggie kissed Nugget good-night and slipped into her own room to get ready for bed.

The light in the living room was off, so Maggie guessed that R.J. had gone to bed, also. She was glad. She didn't want his company while he was in such a black mood. Still she wondered why the date with Darla had been cut short.

Her face finally cleaned of makeup, Maggie began brushing her hair, only to remember she'd left the top down on her car. There hadn't been a drop of rain since she'd been in Texas, but there could possibly be a miracle and she would hate her car's interior to be ruined.

Not bothering to pull a robe over her gown, she slipped out of the house by way of the kitchen. There was a half moon, and the light it shed made it easy for Maggie to find the latches that secured the vinyl top. She was just rolling up the passenger window when the crunch of footsteps sounded behind her.

Whirling around in fright, one hand clinging to her bare throat, she gasped, "R.J., you scared the wits out of me!"

He didn't say anything, just stood watching her, taking in her appearance in the white satin gown, its soft material clinging to her body and the dainty lace framing the cleft of her bosom.

When his silence continued and the race of her heart had slowed, she asked, "What are you doing out here? I thought you were in bed."

He took a step toward her and it brought him out of the shadows. Maggie swallowed at the sight of his chest and shoulders gleaming beneath the moonbeams.

"I've been waiting," he stated flatly.

Maggie's eyes widened on his face. "Waiting? For what?"

His mouth was suddenly an ironic twist beneath the sable mustache. "For you," he answered.

Chapter Nine

Me?'' Maggie repeated softly. Her heart gave a lurch, then sped on in a fast erratic beat that made her hands tremble. "Why?"

R.J. was suddenly looming over her, and she was trapped as he leaned his weight against the car, an arm at either side of her waist. "Because I want to know what kind of game you're playing."

"Game?" Maggie echoed once again. She looked up into his face, which was now only inches from hers. "I think you've gone mad!"

"I think I have, too," he replied. "In fact, that's the way you want it, isn't it? You're doing everything you can think of to get back at me for not playing kiss and touch, for not becoming one more of Maggie's men."

Furious, Maggie slapped him. "You're no outlaw, R.J.; you're a swine of the first degree," she gritted.

His smile was cruel. "I've been called worse things before and lived through it."

"Yes, but did the other guy?"

He chuckled. "Clever girl."

"Not really," she snapped. "I still don't have the slightest idea what you're talking about."

One of his hands lifted to touch her hair, and Maggie involuntarily shivered as the rough palm ran over the silky strands then stopped when it reached her throat. "You've been avoiding me like the plague," he said.

Maggie's breaths were so shallow that she wasn't even sure she was breathing. "That's because you wanted it that way, remember?"

"I also remember telling you that I wanted you to eat, to gain weight, and you have." His hands closed about her rib cage and she felt her heart going out of control as his thumb moved over the curve of her breast. "I suggested you cut your hair, and now you have. Are you telling me you haven't done it for my benefit?"

"No—no I haven't," she denied. "And I'm sorry you don't like my appearance," she whispered as an afterthought.

"You're not sorry," he told her. "You've made sure I like everything about you. Your hair, your clothes, the way you walk and talk, your beautiful body. Oh, yes," he drawled in a husky whisper, "your body looks like a real woman's now. I'm just wondering how much you really want from me."

Maggie studied his face as his hands moved over her breast, then slid slowly, ever so slowly, down her waist until his hands cupped the curve of her bottom. "I...I don't want anything from you," she said on a breathless note. Right now there was some truth to her words. He wasn't behaving like the R.J. she knew, the R.J. she loved with every fiber of her being.

"I can't believe that, Maggie. Everything you've done these past few weeks belies your words."

"You must be drunk," she accused.

"We both know I'm not." His softly spoken words caused a sensual shiver to ripple through Maggie.

"Then you must have gone crazy," she gasped, pressing her palms against his chest in an effort to ward him off.

"No, my dear. I've merely decided to give you what you want."

"And what do I want?" she taunted. "How could you possibly know? You're nothing but a Texas cow—"

"You're right, Miss Maggie," he interrupted. "I'm not one of those pansies back in New York that you lead around by the nose. Believe me, when I take a woman to bed I know what to do with her."

"No doubt," she jeered. "I'm sure you've had plenty of experience."

"I don't think you'll be disappointed."

Maggie wanted to hate him for reminding her that he had made love to other women. She wanted to—but her heart wasn't listening. Already it was beating out a rapid thud of desire at his nearness. "That hardly matters because I have no intention of letting you prove your prowess as a lover to me."

Before Maggie knew what was happening, he swung her up into his arms, his laughter fanning her cheeks. "We'll see," he growled.

"Put me down," she cried as he began to stride off with her.

When he didn't comply Maggie began to struggle by pummeling his shoulders with her fist.

"What's the matter, Maggie? Now that you're near the fire, are you afraid of getting burned?" he taunted.

She strained indignantly against him, while inwardly she marveled at his strength. He was carrying her as if she weighed no more than Nugget. And the smug man wasn't even breathing hard!

"No! It's just that when I do decide to make love, it won't be with a swine like you!"

"God, you should be in the movies." He laughed. "I've never seen such a convincing actress."

Before she could utter a retort, he dropped her onto the cushioned chaise longue. Maggie felt utterly lost as his hard body came down on her, pinning her between him and the chair.

His profile was a beautiful thing in the moonlight, and the sight of it wrenched her heart. How she'd dreamed of his face drawing down to hers, love and desire for her glowing in his tawny eyes. But that was not the case. He only wanted to hurt her. Why, she didn't really know. The only reason she could gather from his words was that he considered her to be teasing and taunting him. If she was guilty of the crime, she'd done it unconsciously. It was true that she wanted him, and maybe unknowingly her desire was so strong that it communicated itself to him. But just how she wanted him was the part he didn't understand. She wanted his love, his real love. Obviously that idea had never entered his head. Maybe that was because he wasn't capable of loving anyone, except Nugget. Maybe *love* was a word R. J. Buchanan didn't know existed.

Maggie was almost sure of that last thought as his lips came down on hers. The idea caused her to struggle in an effort to break away from his embrace.

"R.J., please don't do this. Darla—" she gasped once her lips were free of his.

His expression was hard as he interrupted. "Darla has nothing to do with you and me. You should be worried about Roger. You've had the poor guy going around in a daze all week. But then I guess you're so used to men falling all over you that one more heart to your collection means nothing!"

Did he really think that of her? The idea was painful. She had thought that at least he liked her as a person. Apparently she had deceived herself.

"Then you shouldn't be in danger of becoming one of my victims. You don't even possess a heart!"

He laughed, running his hand over the soft mound of her breast. Maggie could feel the heat of his fingers through the flimsy material of her nightgown, and her body ached with an uncontrollable longing.

"I don't need a heart to give you what you want."

"You're despicable," she lashed out at him as unbidden tears glazed her eyes.

"Maybe," he conceded, his lips dipping down to the cleft between her breasts. "But after watching you work, I'm sure you have me beaten by far."

Maggie gasped, both from his words and the touch of his mouth against the soft fullness of her breast. The brush of his mustache followed every little movement of his lips, intensifying the pleasure that shot through her like a poison arrow.

"You're wrong—oh, please, R.J., don't do this. Why do you want to hurt me?"

Her question brought his face up, and Maggie's breath caught in her throat as the angry glitter in his eyes met the doubt in hers. "Maybe it's because I realized today that hurting me has been your intention all along, and now you're using one of my best friends to do it."

"But that's crazy! I have no interest in Roger, other than as a friend," she argued.

"Exactly," he replied, his fingers closing around her waist, making Maggie wonder how his touch could feel so wonderful while his words were so condemning. "Just like I know you have no real interest in me or any other man and probably never will. Tell me, Maggie, how many wounded fools have you left behind?"

Maggie studied his face in the moonlight, and her heart ached with love for him and ached with the pain his gross misjudgments brought.

"Why should you care? From what I hear, you're the playboy of Amarillo, so I'm sure you have my record beaten by far," she cried, her voice rising shrilly. "Remember, you don't want—"

His fingertips touched her lips, halting the rest of her sentence, and his face drew so close to Maggie's that his breath was a warm cloud against her cheeks.

"That's where you're wrong. I do want. I've wanted from the day I first saw you, God help me! I curse the day George made out his will!"

"No more than I!" Maggie shot back after she had jerked her lips away from his touch. "I think the man was literally mad to bring me out here close to you! He knew my taste in men didn't run toward good-time, uncouth—"

"You're wrong about that." He suddenly chuckled, then his lips were against hers, moving with soft deliberation as he spoke. "I'm going to show you just where your taste does run."

"No," Maggie whimpered, knowing if he kissed her she would totally lose all self-control.

Her plea went unheeded. R.J.'s lips closed over hers in a slow seductive search that caused Maggie to grow limp with desire. The invasion of his tongue was welcome, and she wound her arms around him, the last of her resistance ebbing away like the ripple on a lake.

Maggie hated the fact that he could manipulate her so easily. But her love for him made her susceptible and tonight she wanted above all else to have him for herself. To be able to know that at least for a while that he belonged to her, that tonight it wouldn't be Darla or some other woman he was making love to, it would be Maggie.

At the first sign of her response, she could feel him draw away as if he wanted to change his mind, but as her fingers slid around the steel cords of his neck, he moaned in resignation and the warmth of his lips touched hers once again.

"I can't decide whether you're a beautiful angel or a tempting witch. Which are you, Maggie, love?" he asked as he brushed little butterfly kisses across her cheeks, her eyes, her nose.

"Neither," she whispered. "I'm just a woman who wants you."

After that, they both surrendered to the explosive chemistry between them. Maggie didn't understand why this man above all others should produce such a mindless ecstasy in her. Men had kissed and held her before, but none of them, not even Mario, had produced this reckless desire inside her that made her throw all pride and caution to the wind. It was crazy and it was wonderful and she loved him with all her being. It would be impossible for her to turn away.

Slowly, as if savoring each moment, he pushed the gown down over her shoulders, baring her breasts to him and the moonlight. Maggie shivered in the hot night air, her body tensed with longing as she waited for his touch.

When his dark head bent and his lips closed over her sweet nipple, she gasped with exhilaration and threaded her fingers through his silky hair.

"Maggie! You're so beautiful. Too beautiful for any man to resist," he whispered hoarsely as his lips left her breast and traveled with sensual languor across her collarbone.

The feel of his body next to hers was hypnotic. Her mind etched into memory every line of him—the bulge of muscles on his arms and chest, the narrow flatness of his waist, the long corded strength of his thighs as they pressed against hers. In a heady daze, she tried to drink in the spicy smell of him, every sight that surrounded them, every kiss, every caress that passed between them.

She wanted to say *I love you, R.J. I want you forever and always*, but the fear that he would not want to hear such serious declarations held back her words. And then it hit her that he wasn't touching her or kissing her out of love. In his mind, he was only paying her back because he thought she was playing a teasing game. A declaration of love would only bring a mocking laugh to his lips.

The idea was more than her heart could bear. A sob wrenched from her throat and she shoved his shoulders, desperate to get away from his captivating touch.

R.J. was taken completely off guard by the sudden change in Maggie. When she pulled away from him, he stared after her in complete bewilderment.

"Maggie? What...?"

She didn't stop to hear his words; she only knew she had to escape from him, escape this overwhelming desire to give herself to him before it was too late.

Once she was locked in the dark security of her bedroom, the tears began to flow hot and heavy. She sank down on the carpet and let her head drop against the windowsill. The tears were useless, she knew, but still she could not stop them.

"Maggie, let me in."

R.J.'s whispered command followed by the rattling of her doorknob startled her, and she jumped to her feet to stare at the door as if she expected to see him coming through it any minute.

"Maggie, I know you can hear me. Open this door."

She ignored him and fell across the bed, turning her face against the mattress so he couldn't hear her sobs. She was certain he would go away in a minute. He wouldn't take the chance of making too much noise and waking Nugget.

Her conclusion was correct, for in a few moments she could hear his muffled footsteps moving away from the door. That was why it was such a shock when only a second later she heard the window next to the bed gently sliding up.

In horror, she watched R.J. climb through her bedroom window as if it was a normal, everyday occurrence. Hysterical laughter welled up inside her as he pushed the window down and turned to face her. This couldn't be happening to her!

"Why didn't you open the door?" he demanded.

She scooted off the bed, feeling as if it was the most dangerous place she could be right now. "Because I didn't want to," she blurted, slowly backing away from him.

"Why? So you could make me beg? Now that you know how much I want you, you're going to hold it over me?"

His words did nothing but confuse her, and she buried her face in her hands. "Want me? God, R.J.! Haven't you humiliated me enough for one night?"

"You call that humiliating? Come on, Maggie. You weren't exactly unresponsive, you know."

Her whole body burned at his words, but she did not outwardly acknowledge them. After a few, silent seconds ticked by, she heard him sigh and looked up to see him moving toward her.

"So you're a good lover. I'll admit that," she retorted, feeling the need to stab him with indifference.

"Do you always respond to a man like that just because he's a good lover?" he asked, and from the dismay in his voice, Maggie knew she had wounded him. "If that's true, then everything you said about your innocence is a flat-out lie. Do you know how close we were to making love?"

Maggie stared at him, all the confusion and pain she was feeling evident in the expression on her beautiful features. The concern she found on his face confused her even more and her lower lip began to tremble. Unable to stop herself, she fell against his chest, sobbing weakly.

"Shh, don't cry, Maggie girl," he whispered, his hand gently stroking her hair. "I didn't really want to hurt you. I just—"

Maggie stirred at his hesitation and lifted her head to look at him. The solid strength and beauty of his face tugged her heart. She wondered what was going on behind those lion-brown eyes and she wanted to say, *What, R.J.? What had been on your mind while you held me in such rapturous splendor?*

His fingertips touched her face, traced the anxious wrinkles from her brow, outlined her eyes, her nose and finally her mouth. As his finger brushed against her kiss-swollen lips, it was all she could do to keep from turning her mouth against the rough skin of his palm.

"Neither one of us should be trying to hurt the other, not when we know it can be beautiful between us. Let's face it, Maggie, whether you want it, or I want it, there's something between us that can't be denied. God knows I've tried hard enough! I told you I could keep my hands off you. I told you it would be easy, but you must have known even then that I was lying through my teeth!"

His words shook her to the core, and her hands fluttered against his chest. "What do you mean?" she whispered.

"It means," he purred in his throat, "that I want you, that I've wanted you from the start. And it means we're going to have to take another look at our relationship."

Maggie opened her mouth to question him, but he cut her off by saying, "I know you're one kind of person and I'm another kind of person. I know when the time comes, it'll be hard to watch you leave. But right now I think I'd walk across hell on a piece of thread just to kiss you again."

"R.J."

His whispered name came out as a wanton plea, and then suddenly she was crushed in his tight embrace, returning his kisses with all the love she felt for him.

Long minutes passed before R.J. finally pulled away from her. His breathing was quick and ragged when he spoke.

"I think I'd better get out of here before things get out of hand."

Maggie could not keep the yearning look from her face as her eyes met his. She wanted him so! Already he seemed a part of her.

"I'll see you in the morning, okay?"

Maggie nodded as his fingers caressed her cheek, but there were tears in her eyes as she watched him go out the door.

* * *

Bright sunshine was streaming through the window when Maggie finally awoke the next morning. Even then it had not been the glaring light slanting across her bed that had awakened her. It was Nugget standing beside her pillow with a cup of coffee in her hand.

Maggie frowned and reached for the cup as she sat up in bed.

"Oh, Nugget," she moaned, "What time is it?"

"Nearly ten."

"Ten! Where—" Maggie was suddenly wide awake. "Where is your daddy?"

Nugget smiled as if she thought Maggie's question a very strange one. "At work. He said that you were tired and to let you sleep for a while."

Maggie plopped the coffee cup down on the nightstand and hastily scrambled out of bed. "Nugget, you shouldn't have let me sleep *this* late!" she exclaimed, grabbing her robe and heading toward the shower.

As the hot water pelted her skin, Maggie had to admit she felt a little puzzled and hurt that R.J. hadn't wakened her before he left for work.

You're a stupid romantic fool, Maggie Winslow, she berated herself. R. J. Buchanan had to be a man without principles. What other kind of man would take one woman out on a date, then come home and make advances to another one? And what did that make her? A woman so desperate for a man she would stoop to anything?

No, she silently cried. It hadn't been like that for her. She didn't know what R.J. was feeling after last night's exchange of passion, but she had responded to him only because she loved him. Indeed, it was far too much to ever expect that he might return that love. But surely the man couldn't have kissed her so intently, so passionately, and not at least had *some* feelings toward her.

This idea lifted her spirits somewhat and she dressed hurriedly but with care. She hoped he'd still be at the office by the time she got there. She wanted to see him so badly that it was almost a physical pain.

R.J. was on the telephone when Maggie and Nugget arrived in his office. At their entrance, he swiveled the desk chair and threw her a frosty look.

"Here she is now," he said into the mouthpiece, then handed the receiver to Maggie.

A sinking sensation rushed through her. She'd expected R.J. to greet her warmly, the memory of their kisses revealed in his eyes. Instead, she saw a cold man who practically stared a hole through her.

"Hello?" she answered, expecting her mother to be on the other end. She was the only one who knew where to reach her.

"Maggie, dear, your voice sounds wonderful."

"Phillip!" she gasped, unable to hide her shock at hearing his voice, then added angrily, "I see you've been harming mother again."

"Maggie, love, that's not a very nice greeting. I was hoping to hear something like 'It's great to hear your voice, I miss you, Phillip, darling.'"

Maggie glanced at R.J., half afraid that he could hear Phillip's words. Why she should worry about such a thing, she wasn't quite sure. She just knew she felt uncomfortable with his cool amber eyes watching her closely while Phillip's gushing voice continued.

"Sorry to disappoint you. I just wasn't expecting to hear from you." From the corner of her eye, she saw R.J.'s mouth twist into a mocking sneer, and she fidgeted nervously with the curly telephone line.

"I'll forgive you, darling, just as soon as I meet you at the airport."

"Airport? What do you mean?"

He chuckled, letting her know that he was sure of his hold
on her. "It means you've already overstayed your vacation. I need you back here, for more than one reason."

"I'm not ready to come back to work." Not now, her
heart cried, not when she was just learning what it was like
to love someone, to live not just for herself, but for someone else.

"*Vogue* is crying for you."

Maggie sighed impatiently. "*Vogue* has cried before."

"So forget *Vogue*," he said so swiftly that Maggie was
suddenly suspicious. "I have something far more interesting."

"I'm not interested—not right now."

R.J. stood up and went across the room to pour himself
a cup of coffee. Nugget was already settled in a little nook,
her crayons and coloring book spread out before her.

"Don't be ridiculous. Leon Benetti wants you for a film.
Now say no," he dared.

Inwardly, Maggie was surprised at this bit of news. Benetti was a famous film producer, his work highly re-
spected. It was incredible that a man of his talent would
want her for a part.

"Phillip, that's crazy! I have no training for something
like that!"

"You don't have to be an actress."

"That's what I thought—just a bunch of nude shots."

"Don't jump to conclusions. You won't be nude. And
you *will* have a few lines. With a good director, you'll be
great. Just think, Maggie, what kind of exposure you'll get,
what a magnificent opportunity it would give you toward an
acting career! You should feel highly honored that Benetti
is asking for you!"

Nugget's little head was bent over the coloring book and
Maggie studied her shining curls. The child had captured a
place in her heart, and she could not imagine waking up
without the little girl's bright, cheerful face, her kisses and

ugs, her constant chatter on ever-changing subjects.
Without volition, her eyes swung to R.J., and she swallowed painfully as she gazed at the strong lines of his back
and shoulders. She loved him. It was incredible just how
much. And with Phillip on the other end of the line, she re-
lized how complicated, how impossible it would be for
their lives to fit together if she remained a model.

"Naturally, I am honored. But I just don't think—"

"Maggie, my sweet, get a flight tomorrow. I'll meet you
at the airport. Benetti is expecting us the middle of the week.
We'll fly out to L.A. on Wednesday."

"Don't push me, Phillip," she warned.

"Darling, I'm not pushing. I'm insisting."

"I'll think about it," she hedged. "Now I really must go."

"I'll call you tomorrow," he assured her, then added in
domineering tone, "by the way, who does the forceful
voice belong to?"

A hysterical sob rose in her throat, and she wanted to cry,
*he's my friend and my lover, the man I want to spend the
rest of my life with, but he doesn't want or need a long range
commitment.* Especially not when he has Darla waiting patiently for a marriage proposal.

"It shouldn't matter to you," she evaded his question.

He let out an impatient breath. "Just remember New
York is your home. You know where your bread is buttered."

Maggie slammed down the receiver with a vengeance, and
as she looked up to meet R.J.'s suspicious gaze, tears sparkled her blue eyes.

He opened his mouth to speak, but Maggie rushed toward the door. She couldn't let him see her cry!

She was running down the corridor toward the ladies'
room when R.J.'s hand clamped down on her shoulder.

"Wait, Maggie," he said.

"Leave me alone!" she gritted, pushing through the door
an effort to escape.

She was flabbergasted when R.J. followed her, and sh
was grateful the facilities weren't occupied.

She whirled on him. "Good Lord, can't I even have fiv
minutes to myself?"

His fingers caught her chin and tilted her face up for hi
inspection. "You may have five minutes whenever you wish
But not to fret over some obnoxious wimp."

"Damn you men! Damn all men!" she shouted at him
"You call Phillip obnoxious, but you're just like him. Yo
both think you know all about me—how I feel—where
belong. But you don't! Neither one of you!"

Angry tears spilled onto her cheeks, and she wiped a
them furiously.

"Maggie, Maggie," he murmured gently. His fingers le
her chin and slid distractingly down her throat, then curve
around the base of it. "What's the matter, hmm? Do yo
want to go back to New York? Has this guy made you re
gret what happened between us last night?"

She searched his face, trying to decide if the question
were really sincere. "No," she whispered with an emphati
shake of her head.

He let out a breath and moved closer so that his cheek wa
resting against hers. "I should feel terrible about la
night—but I can't."

His arms moved around her and Maggie melted again
him. This was where she belonged. How could he not kno
it! Not feel it!

"I'm sorry I greeted you so curtly. It wasn't what I ha
planned, but your agent was the last person I wanted to ta
to this morning."

"Me too," she admitted shakily. "Whatever you mig
think, I'm not romantically involved with him."

His fingers moved softly, rhythmically against her bac
"I'm thankful for that much. But, Maggie, I . . . Phillip S
ville's phone call made me realize just how far apart o
lives really are—"

"Why don't you let me decide that!" She pulled away
from him determinedly, and her eyes dared him to argue the
matter. "Like I told you, you don't know what I want."

"Neither do you," he countered.

"How do you know?" she shot back.

"How do I know?" he echoed sharply. "Since you are a
virgin, it's obvious you're not the kind of woman who takes
lovemaking casually. And last night's kisses were hardly
casual.

"So what does that prove?" she spat at him. She was
fiercely angry because he could not understand that she was
eaten up with love for him.

"It proves that you haven't thought anything through,"
he answered, his hands curving over her shoulders with a
firm grip. "You came out here on a whim for a simple vacation. I don't want you getting involved in something that
you'll regret later on. I don't want you to be hurt. And I
damned well don't want to be the one to hurt you." He
shook his head rather helplessly.

"Don't tell me you're going to apologize for last night!"
she accused.

Whatever he had been going to say was cut off as Maggie
went on heatedly. "I'm twenty-four years old, R.J., not a
child. But like Phillip, you think I'm without a brain, that
I'm unable to make a rational decision of any kind, that if
someone doesn't lead me around by the nose I'll get lost!
Well, I—"

"Shh—" His soft voice interrupted her furious tirade.
"Maggie, darling, don't say such foolish things," he
pleaded gently. "You've got to stop and realize that you're
unique, you're not like Helen or Darla or any woman here
in Amarillo or even most women in New York. You've got
a highly successful career, and you're internationally recognized. That's not something to take lightly."

Her anger began to drain away as she listened to hi
words. He was right on one point, but blind to so many
others.

"I'm not taking it lightly, R.J."

His mouth twisted in disbelief. "Maybe not, but you can'
deny you're getting involved with the life here in Amarillo
with Nugget, with me."

She swallowed, suddenly realizing what he was trying t
get at. He didn't want her developing serious thoughts abou
their relationship. He didn't want to get *that* involved.

"And you wouldn't like that," she finished, her voic
betrayingly despondent.

"Maggie, I didn't say that!" he muttered. He grabbed he
waist and pulled her tightly against his hard male body
"I'm just saying I'll be the last person to ask you to give u
your career."

Despite his words, Maggie's arms went around his nec
and her fingers slid through the springy waves at the back o
his head. She was totally captivated by him, even knowin
his attentions were merely sexual. "I know that. So why ar
we arguing?" she asked simply.

"Maggie, Maggie," he groaned against her lips. "Why d
you do this to me?"

Even if she had wanted to answer it would have been im
possible. His lips were on hers, heavily, all-consumingly
sending a weak, giddy sensation to every portion of he
body.

Maggie clung to him, finding that his touch threw her int
such a delirious state that she totally forgot their surround
ings. She only knew that his hands were pressing her hip
against his, making her aware of his desire and the meltin
fire in her own blood.

A sudden draft of air, the click of a heel and all at onc
R.J. and Maggie were staring half dazed at a red-face
woman in the doorway.

R.J. was the first to collect himself. He grabbed Maggie by the hand. "Sorry, Loretta," he apologized wryly as he pulled Maggie, who was by now back to her senses and totally mortified, behind him and out the door.

Chapter Ten

"How would you girls like to go on a little trip?" R.J. asked at the supper table that evening.

He had helped Maggie cook chicken and rice for their meal. As she had been helping him at the office, in turn he was helping her with the chores at home. Maggie found his presence in the kitchen sheer joy. A woman would have to be crazy not to enjoy cooking with a man like R.J.

"Where to?" Nugget responded. "Palo Duro?"

"Sorry, dumplin', but not this time. I have a feeling your grandmother wants to see you."

For a moment Nugget's face fell, then just as quickly she brightened. "Is Maggie going with us?" she asked excitedly.

"Of course she's going," he answered smoothly, as Maggie studied him beneath her lowered lashes. She'd never expected him to take her to his parents'. She did her best not to read anything special into it. It was likely that he didn't want her staying here alone.

"Can we go to the beach?"

"I wouldn't think of missing it," he answered before biting into a dinner roll.

Nugget squirmed excitedly on her seat. "Oh, Maggie, this is going to be great. You're going to love it!"

"Whoa," R.J. interjected. "Maggie's probably already been to Corpus Christi. This may be nothing new to her."

Nugget glanced anxiously from her daddy to Maggie. "Have you, Maggie?"

"No, I haven't, Nugget. So you can show me all the sights," she said, smiling at the child.

"Oooh, I can't wait," she cried. "And Grandma and Grandpa Buchanan are going to love you, just like me and daddy do."

Maggie had to drop her gaze and she pretended an interest in the food as she asked, "How long will we be gone?"

She could feel R.J. watching her. "We'll be back by Tuesday. Helen would kill me if we weren't here for their party."

"That's true," Maggie agreed. "And I did promise to help her organize everything."

She wasn't going to mention that Phillip was expecting her to go to L.A. to see Benetti. She wanted to forget she had a life apart from this one. If R.J. knew about the film offer, he would probably ship her off to New York tomorrow, and that was the last thing she wanted.

They left at five the next morning. Their luggage was packed in the trunk of the Mustang, and Nugget was settled in the back seat with an array of dolls and toys to keep her entertained. She had wanted to bring Walter along, but that was one passenger R.J. had balked about taking.

"Do you have a grudge against flying?" she asked as the classic little car sped through the early morning dawn.

R.J. took his eyes momentarily off the road to give her a wry smile. "Still trying to find that psychological hang-up?"

Maggie chuckled. "No, just curious. You've got to admit it's a terribly long drive."

"That's true," he agreed, settling in a more comfortable position behind the wheel. "But I'm young and strong, unless you haven't noticed. And you can't see the countryside, or the people, or the buildings, looking down at a bunch of white fluff," he tacked on with a grin. "But to satisfy that curiosity of yours, yes, I do fly, when the occasion warrants."

Maggie glanced back at Nugget. How could she stand to see him board a plane, as her real parents had been killed in one? Maggie doubted that she could. R.J. deserved credit, she knew, for he had raised Nugget so that she had no undue fears or inhibitions. In fact, she was just like him—intelligent, well-rounded and contented with herself.

"He's not telling you the real reason, Maggie," Nugget spoke up confidently. "He always drives so that we can have the Mustang to go cruisin' in."

"Aha—so she's on to you," Maggie said, throwing him a coy sidelong glance.

R.J. smiled broadly and looked back at his daughter's scheming face. "Well, we can't cruise in your grandmother's Mercedes, can we?"

Nugget giggled. "No way! We want the top down so all the boys will look at us, don't we, Maggie?"

Maggie gave R.J. a conspiratorial wink. "By all means," she agreed earnestly.

It was an all-day drive to Corpus Christi. Maggie expected to get tired but as the day progressed, she found herself enjoying every minute of the trip. It was like a foreign country to her and she enjoyed having R.J. tell her the history of the area and Nugget excitedly point out places of interest. It was incredible to know they could drive for twelve hours and still be in the state of Texas!

The sun had not yet set when they reached the city. Maggie wasn't a bit surprised when R.J. began winding the Mustang through an obviously grand residential area. She would have been surprised the first time she'd seen him at

Tony's if someone had told her he had been raised in this environment. The memory of what she'd thought of him actually tinged her face with color.

"What are you thinking?" he asked, startling Maggie out of her thoughts.

She looked sheepish and even redder as she turned to look at him. "You wouldn't want to know."

"Why?"

"I called you something very disrespectful the first time I met you," she admitted none too proudly.

He chuckled. "So? I called you a skinny red lobster."

"I know."

R.J. threw his daughter an accusing look and Nugget shrugged her shoulders. "It just slipped out," she said, defending herself.

"Yeah, well, I'll remember, young lady."

A few seconds later R.J. was pulling in front of a gorgeous split-level white brick home. Tropical plants filled the yard, and Maggie guessed that the warm climate here on the gulf never varied much.

A Mexican housekeeper named Teresa met them at the door, but they were hardly past the foyer when Maggie caught the sound of another voice.

"R.J.?"

The question was followed by the hurried tap of heels against Spanish tile, then a beautiful woman in her mid-fifties appeared in the doorway.

"R.J.—darling," she hurried toward his outstretched arms. "This is such a pleasant surprise!"

The woman received his embrace with a radiant smile, then bent to kiss Nugget's cheek. What a lovely, elegant woman, Maggie thought. Her olive complexion was moist and smooth, her sable brown hair, barely threaded with silver, was styled into a sleek upswept style. She was wearing a blue paisley skirt and coordinating tank top. Maggie was dismayed by her youthfulness.

"So this is the Maggie I've been hearing so much about," she said, reaching with both hands to Maggie. "I must say, you're absolutely stunning! Your photographs do not do you justice."

Maggie smiled warmly at R.J.'s mother, whose grip was soft, but warm and welcoming. "You're too kind, Mrs. Buchanan," Maggie murmured, wondering how much the woman had actually heard about her and who had told her.

"Oh, call me Sara," she insisted and quickly turned to the housekeeper. "Teresa, please fix some margaritas. Emmaline, what would you like?"

"Kool-aid!" Nugget cried, already skipping around her grandmother and hurrying after Teresa's retreating back.

"I hope you weren't planning on entertaining this weekend. I didn't call because I wanted to surprise you," R.J. said once they were comfortably relaxed in the den, sipping the tangy margaritas.

Maggie glanced discreetly around her surroundings as she listened to R.J. and his mother. The house was furnished in a tropical style and spotlessly clean. As her shoulders sank more deeply into the back of the luxurious couch, Maggie realized that she preferred R.J.'s home. It had a much warmer, homier appeal. Sometimes all three of them snuggled onto the couch together and shared a bowl of popcorn in front of the TV set. She couldn't see that happening in this house.

"I suppose Dad is at the office." R.J. said, a wry note in his voice.

"Yes, he's got an important case coming up Monday. He'll be glad to see you, though," his mother assured him.

Maggie watched R.J.'s mouth hint at a smile before he brought the cocktail glass up to his lips. "Yes, he'll enjoy seeing his son and granddaughter. But not quite as much as winning his next case."

"Oh, R.J.," Sara reproved. "You're so blunt and it's not really like that—"

"No, it's not. You're right," he interrupted his mother with a beguiling smile. "It's just that his career dominates him. I'm just thankful I turned out like you, Mother." He winked at Maggie, who was sitting only inches away from him. "Tell her, Maggie, how much I worry about my business and how often I work late!"

For a moment Maggie was nonplussed, for both statements couldn't have been further from the truth. "I have never known you to worry about your business nor have I seen you work late," she answered truthfully.

"Has he coached you to say these things?" Mrs. Buchanan asked teasingly. "He doesn't want me to worry about him. But I do. He tries to make me believe his business isn't demanding, but I'm not that foolish. And then to be raising Emmaline all alone—"

R.J. shook his head in a scolding manner at Sara. "Mother, Nugget is a joy, not a job. She's my daughter."

A shadow formed on Sara's face and she took a deep breath. Maggie watched the other woman fiddle with her cocktail glass and knew she was probably thinking of the son she had lost and the protective love she could not help but feel for R.J.

"I didn't mean—but, well, you could use help."

R.J. chuckled. "What do you think Maggie is, an ornament?"

Sara gasped and gave him a pointed look. "No, smartaleck boy. But she'll be going back to New York fairly soon, won't you, Maggie?"

Sara Buchanan looked at Maggie for an answer, and Maggie glanced over at R.J. She wanted to cry that she never wanted to go back, but knew that would shock and embarrass everyone. Besides, the dark scowl on R.J.'s face gave her the answer.

"Yes, I'll be going back later on this summer." She tried to keep her tone light, but the lump in her throat made it very difficult. "But I wouldn't worry about R.J., Sara,"

Maggie went on. "He's not a candidate for an ulcer. In fact, when I first met him, he infuriated me because he seemed so contented."

R.J. threw her a sidelong glance that seemed to ask, How do you know I'm contented? But before Maggie could think about it, Sara was laughing heartily.

"I'm sure your life as a model must be very stressful—quite a contrast to R.J.'s. Leo says he would lose his mind living where R.J. does. What do you think about it?"

Maggie's forefinger circled the rim of her glass. She knew that R.J. would be weighing her response. "At first I thought it was a godforsaken desert. Then R.J. showed me it really was a very rich, productive farming country. It's incredible what they do with irrigation. But what fascinates me most about the area is the wide-open space. I never knew there were so many stars. Living in the city, one finds it's hard to see the sky for the buildings and the smog."

"I'm glad you're enjoying your visit to Texas. I must say from Nugget's letters she's fallen in love with you."

Maggie could not help but glance at R.J., and a warm feeling spread through her as his heavy-lidded gaze met hers. He looked very suave and handsome wearing chocolate-colored slacks and a brown pin-striped dress shirt. She had finally gotten used to the extreme contrast of his appearance. It was nothing for him to go from jeans and boots to a business suit. Sitting beside him in the sumptuous surroundings, she decided without a doubt that the R.J. she loved was the one in a pair of Levi's and boots, his head stuck under the hood of a car, his bare shoulders glistening with sweat and a grin on his face.

"She's a pure joy. I think I love her more than she does me," Maggie acknowledged. *And I love her daddy even more,* she wanted to say. She wondered if Sara Buchanan would be surprised at such a statement, or had she been visited by many of R.J.'s girlfriends? Maggie didn't really want to know the answer to that question. She liked to imagine she was the only woman who had made a visit to Corpus Christi.

"I'm sure she'll be heartsick when you have to leave," Sara said, "but in your type of work it's probably difficult to get away for any length of time."

Maggie nodded. "This is the first real vacation I've had since I became a model. And I only got this one because I was so determined to take one."

"You know I've been curious about something ever since you walked in the door," Sara confessed.

"Oh, what is it?" Maggie asked.

"Your hair. In all your photos, it's always been so long. Is the short style a new promotional thing?"

Sara's words caused Maggie's eyes to swing over to R.J., and they exchanged glances that said neither one of them was going to forget the uproar her haircut had brought about.

"Not actually," she hedged. "It...it's just so terribly hot in this part of the country that I thought it would be more comfortable."

Sara smiled with understanding. "Yes, unfortunately the Texas heat can be extreme. But your hair looks lovely."

Maggie threw another glance at R.J. before she extended Sara a soft "Thank you."

The evening turned out to be a very pleasant one for Maggie. They had to hold off dinner for more than forty minutes in order for Leo Buchanan to make it back from the law office. Both R.J. and his mother didn't appear put out by the delay, but rather seemed to expect it.

They passed the time with R.J. and Nugget playing the piano. Maggie knew that R.J. was an accomplished player because he worked with Nugget at home every night before bedtime. But what she didn't know was that playing the piano was something R.J. had hated as a child, or so Sara told her. Still, his mother had insisted on the lessons, anyway.

"I made him continue with the lessons because he had real talent for it, not just because I was one of those mothers who expected their children to learn to play a musical instrument, no matter the cost," Sara said, defending her actions.

R.J. chuckled as his fingers skimmed over the ivory keys. "I'll never forget, Mother, that time I had to miss a baseball game because fluffy-headed Sally Wentworth was getting married and I had to play at the ceremony!" R.J. reminisced.

Sara Buchanan laughed at the memory. "Yes, you were furious at me. Especially after your team lost and everyone considered you the star hitter. But on the other hand, there were hundreds at the wedding and they were all talking about your music."

"My baseball coach was really interested in that bit of social news," he said wryly.

"Well," Sara said, smiling over at Maggie. "I'm sure your playing has had some advantages to it."

R.J.'s brows lifted coyly, then he looked at Maggie and his mother with a deadpan expression. "By all means—it enabled me to prove to Maggie that we Texans are really civilized people."

"R.J.—" Maggie gasped, but Sara interrupted her with amused curiosity.

"Oh, really?"

"Naturally. I just played her a few pieces by Chopin and she could see for herself that we weren't all oil wells and cattle down here."

"R.J., you are conceited," Maggie accused. "And just want your mother to believe I was a snob instead of a New Yorker."

"Oh?" R.J. chuckled. "I didn't know there was any difference between the two."

"Oh, R.J.!" Sara reproved while Maggie rose to his bait all too willingly.

"How can you speak of us like that when you've probably never been to New York in your life!"

For a moment he forgot the melody as he turned toward Maggie, a smug, knowing expression on his face. "Don't remind me of my trips to New York City. The last one was hard to beat. There were smog alerts every day I was there, the sanitation department had gone on strike and garbage was piled up on the streets, not to mention the fact that I was solicited right in front of my hotel."

Maggie wanted to retort, but held her tongue because of Nugget's presence. However, his mother said, "Well, R.J., you should have just put it down to your good looks."

He laughed and turned back to the keyboard. "And to think all this time I thought it was my money."

"R.J., please hush and play my favorite. Or have you forgotten it?"

"Never, dear Mom," he assured her and threw Maggie a disarming wink as his fingers came down on the keys.

The famous tune from the movie *Casablanca* filled the room, and Maggie made the mistake of thinking of its romantic words while watching R.J. It put stars in her eyes and she hoped Sara wouldn't notice how much in love she was with her son.

Maggie learned a lot about R.J. as the night progressed, first from his mother and then later when his father, Leo, arrived.

The older Buchanan was completely gray haired, much taller, and of a more slender build than R.J. He was almost austere in appearance, but Maggie suspected that underneath the exterior was a gentle person. At least he treated Maggie with genuine warmth, and it didn't take long to pick up on the respect that flowed between father and son. R.J. had called himself a black sheep, yet she could see for herself that Leo Buchanan was extremely proud of his son.

The next morning the three of them, and Sara, packed a picnic and headed to the beach. The gulf was beautiful and so much warmer compared to the Atlantic Ocean.

Maggie wore a yellow bikini so that she could soak up as much sun as she could, and R.J. teased her by saying she was trying to start a stampede on the beach. Admittedly there were a few men eyeing her, but they were also eyeing the other women around them, too. Maggie scarcely noticed them, anyway.

While Sara helped her granddaughter build sand castles, Maggie and R.J. toasted in the sun and listened to the radio.

Maggie watched Nugget and her grandmother for a long while until the sight of them playing in the sun and sand filled her with sad reflections. Maggie's own mother would have never set foot on a private beach, much less a public one.

Comparing her family to R.J.'s, Maggie realized she had never really had one and how much she would be missing once she had to go back to New York. Who or what would be there to fill the void? The question seemed to be haunting her constantly these days.

They all played in the surf until they were exhausted, then ate sandwiches and fresh fruit from a wicker basket beneath a huge umbrella. Before the day was over, Nugget and Maggie walked for a long distance along the beach, hunting shells and other bits of sea life. They found several keepsakes, and Maggie gave R.J. a delicate little clamshell that was open but still connected in the center.

She hoped he would keep it always, and maybe a long time from now he would look at it and remember their time together.

"Maggie, I hope you're not as tired as Nugget," R.J. commented as Maggie shut the door behind the sleeping child.

"Why?" Maggie asked curiously, running a hand over her hair.

They had just gotten home and she hadn't yet had time to shower the salt and sand away. Nugget had gone to sleep in the car, and rather than wake her, R.J. had carried her in to the bedroom. Maggie had followed like a mother hen to make sure she was properly tucked in.

"Why?" he echoed impatiently. "Because I intend to take you out on the town. You're going to taste the most delicious shrimp you ever ate and then I'm going to dance your legs off."

Maggie groaned even though a thrill of excitement rippled through her at the idea of being alone with him. "Give me time to get ready!"

"One hour, love," he said, chucking her under the chin, then walking toward his own room with a soft little whistle.

Maggie used the next hour to the utmost. Being a model, she could change clothes in a flash and it was a good thing because she changed several times before deciding on one certain look. It was a peach-colored dress of soft challis that did nice things for her tan and light blue eyes. The effort had been all worthwhile she knew as she sat across from R.J. and his eyes glided over her in the dim lighting of the restaurant.

"You look lovely tonight, Maggie. That agent of yours should see you now."

Maggie's faint smile was a bit disbelieving, and she almost wanted to laugh. Yes, Phillip should see her now. Perhaps he wouldn't be so quick to call her back to New York. He would think she was far from lovely with short hair, short nails and the fifteen pounds she'd gained. She could just hear his scathing remarks.

"I'm glad it's you seeing me instead," she answered honestly.

He reached across the table and picked up her hand. Her heart thumped erratically at his touch.

"He wants you to come back to work."

She nodded at the statement, wishing he hadn't brought the subject into their conversation. She was trying so hard to pretend that part of her life didn't exist. "I told him I wasn't ready to go back to work."

"I know. I heard."

She took a deep breath before she met his eyes, and there was a tremulous little smile on her lips. "I don't really want to talk about it."

"No." He sighed rather impatiently. "Neither do I."

It was then the waiter arrived with their order, and Maggie was glad of the diversion. For the next several minutes they were busily enjoying the enormous shrimp caught fresh in the Gulf of Mexico. R.J. was right—she had never tasted anything like it, and she enjoyed the food to the limit.

"Darla won't be too happy when she hears you brought me with you to visit your parents," Maggie surprised herself by saying. "Aren't you afraid she's going to lose her patience with you?"

R.J.'s tawny eyes narrowed on her face as he lifted his wineglass. "Patience," he repeated mockingly. "You've got to be kidding. She doesn't know the word."

Maggie threw him a puzzled look. "Then why do you date her?"

"I don't date Darla, I go out with her. And I only did that to try to get you off my mind. It failed rather pitifully," he admitted ruefully.

"I . . . I thought you planned to marry her!"

He shocked her even more by letting out a low yelp of laughter. "Marry Darla! That *is* a joke. When I marry, I want it to be for love. Darla doesn't know the meaning of love, and she's certainly not the kind of woman I want to be Nugget's mother."

Maggie hoped he couldn't detect her sigh of relief. He might not be serious about her, but at least the supercilious Miss Woods wasn't going to get him.

"Nugget would love to hear that. She hates the woman."

R.J.'s mustache gave a wry little twist. "Nugget never has been very subtle—a very unfeminine trait. Maybe you could help her in that department."

Maggie laughed. "Nugget is just refreshingly frank. Let her be as she is. God knows my own personality has had to take a back seat to a model's image for many years now."

The smile still on his face, R.J. put down his fork and reached for her hand once again. "Well, Maggie Winslow, I'd like you completely uncovered, in more ways than one."

After the meal, they danced several times. The floor was dimly lit, the music slow and sensuous and conducive to romance, or at least Maggie tried to blame her quickening pulse partially on the atmosphere. However, she knew that being in R.J.'s arms was all it took to make her come alive. She was sorry when he suggested they go. She didn't want the night to end.

"Can we drive by the ocean?" she asked once they were traveling along a main thoroughfare.

R.J. had the top down on the Mustang, and the breeze felt wonderful now that the sun had disappeared. Maggie lifted her face to it, shaking her blond waves back behind her.

He smiled indulgently at her purely sybaritic movements. "We can do more than drive by the beach; we'll go down and walk on it. I've always loved the ocean at night, and I know just the place for a walk."

It wasn't long before R.J. was parking the car along a deserted stretch of beach. Maggie left her heels in the car and laughingly ran ahead of him. He caught up to her in a matter of seconds, his arm coming around her waist with the ease of a familiar friend's.

Maggie smiled up at him as she breathed in the salty breeze. It was beautiful there with the moonlight on the water, but it was even more beautiful because he was there, the warmth of his arm spreading a sense of security around her.

"I'll bet you had a hundred girls down here when you were a teenager," she suggested teasingly.

"Jealous, are you?" he replied.

Her arm came around the back of his waist and she rested her head against his shoulder as they strolled along the lapping edge of waves.

"Frightfully," she said with a soft laugh.

She felt more than saw him loosen his necktie so that the ends dangled against his shirt. "You shouldn't be. I was a terrible lover, even though I didn't think so at the time."

She laughed again, and his footsteps halted as he pulled her into his arms. Breathless, she leaned her forehead against his.

"Maybe you just didn't have the right partner," she whispered suggestively.

She could tell by the sound of his voice that he was smiling. "And do you think I have her now?"

Her arms tightened around his lean waist. "I'd like to think so."

He pulled her up closer so that her warm and yielding body was crushed against his. "Maggie, Maggie love, I didn't bring you all the way to Corpus Christi to make love to you. In fact, I brought you down here to keep from it. I wanted to give us both time to think, to— Oh, hell, Maggie, I want you—"

Before she had a chance to think about his words, he lifted her into his arms and her hands locked behind the strong column of his neck.

"All I can think about is making love to you..." he murmured softly as she gazed up at him, her cheek pressed against his shoulder.

"Me too," she admitted shakily.

His tawny eyes reverently scanned the contours of her face before he took her lips beneath his. For long moments Maggie forgot that he was supporting her weight. She only knew that his lips were sending her to a place where there was the taste of him, the warmth of his body, the sound of the wind and waves.

He carried her to a little hidden cove of rocks and eased her gently down onto the warm sand. "Your dress is going to get dirty," he said, his voice husky.

Maggie didn't care if it was completely ruined. She pulled him down next to her. "Forget my dress," she pleaded against his lips.

He laughed softly, his hands reaching for her shoulders, and Maggie smiled up at him in the moonlight. "You're gorgeous, do you know that?" she asked, secretly amazed that she should feel no reticence.

One side of his mustache cocked upward. "No, but I'm glad you like my looks, because I know I sure do like looking at you... touching you."

His voice grew thick, his eyelids heavy and his head bent to hers. "God, Maggie, you make me feel like I'm twenty again. My hands shake when I touch you, my head spins, I forget everything—everything—"

The last words were practically incoherent as Maggie groaned his name and wound her arms around his neck.

She knew that whatever happened she would never forget this night, the warm sand, his lips on hers, spinning the stars above her in a whirlwind of bright sensation. As he held her, Maggie's heart cried over and over that this man was hers, and she was his. How could it be any other way?

Her mind was fighting the battle of that question when suddenly he raised up and planted his hands on the sand at either side of her head. The moon was behind him, outlining his face and shoulders and throwing his features into shadow.

She peered up at his face, trying to see what he was thinking but it was a mystery in the darkness and she was totally unprepared for his words.

"Maggie, I want to marry you. I want you to be my wife."

She sucked in a breath of disbelief and then his name came rushing out. "R.J.! R.J.!" she cried, flinging her arms around his neck.

He clutched her close against him, rocking her to and fro as she sobbed and laughed at the same time.

"I love you, Maggie girl. I never thought I could feel this way about a woman. I never expected to. Now that I do, I can't let you go, even though I know it's going to be hard—"

"Hard?" she repeated quizzically, wiping the tears of joy from her cheeks.

"Yes, you know. With you being a model and with my home and business here in Amarillo. But don't worry about it, darling. We'll work something out. I've never been a city boy, even though I grew up here in Corpus Christi. But I'll live part of the time in New York if I have to."

"R.J.!" She caught his chin with her fingers and held his face so that she could search his eyes for some kind of explanation. "You're talking crazily! There's no need to work anything out. I don't want to be a model anymore. I want to be your wife—Nugget's mother. That's all."

He sighed and his palm curved against her cheek. Maggie rubbed against it with catlike contentment.

"You say that now, Maggie, but you may not feel that way later on. I don't want that. I don't want you to have to give up anything. I want you to be happy, for us to be happy and together."

"We will, R.J. I—"

She started to convince him how certain she was of her decision, yet he interrupted her with a kiss that grew more sensual as the moments passed.

Her back was against the sand, his chest crushed against her breasts when he finally said, "Let's not argue, my love. Just let me enjoy you and this night. Tomorrow we're going home. We'll work it out then."

Maggie didn't argue. It didn't matter. All that mattered was that he loved her. They were going to be married and spend the rest of their lives together. Tomorrow would come soon enough.

Chapter Eleven

Maggie and R.J. decided to wait before telling Nugget and his parents about their decision to marry. They wanted Nugget to be home in familiar surroundings when they gave her the news, and R.J. had laughingly said his mother would have an enormous wedding planned in two hours if he gave her the chance.

The drive back to Amarillo was even more pleasant than the ride down. Maggie was ecstatic. R.J. loved her and she was going to be Nugget's mother, not just a stand-in for the summer. For the first time in her life, she was going to live in a home filled with love.

A couple of times on the way home thoughts of Phillip and the film deal crossed her mind. She didn't bring it up with R.J. She felt sure he wouldn't want to discuss it in front of his daughter, and Maggie considered the whole subject unimportant as far as she was concerned.

Once they got back to Amarillo, she would call Phillip and give him the news that she was retiring. It would certainly cause her no pain to give that up. She hoped she could make R.J. understand. For six years she had been a career woman and several years before that she'd trained for the job. Living with R.J. and Nugget had proved to her that a career did not make her feel loved or needed or important in someone else's life. And she needed that. She needed R.J.'s love more than anything she had ever needed in her life. Perhaps this was what George had tried to tell her so long ago.

Apparently, Maggie and R.J. must have held hands once too often or looked at each other with too many stars in their eyes before they got home because Nugget finally scooted up on the seat and said, "Did you two fall in love while we were in Corpus Christi?"

R.J. laughed and Maggie's eyes showed surprise as they both looked back at Nugget's smiling face.

"How could you tell?" R.J. teased. "And do you know what falling in love is?"

Nugget was offended. "I sure do! It means when a boy and girl like each other a whole lot. They like each other so much that they want to get married and have babies and live together until they die."

R.J. nodded and looked across at Maggie with unexpected seriousness. "I couldn't have said it better, Nugget. That's exactly what it means."

The child suddenly bounced on the seat so hard that her head nearly hit the vinyl roof. "Yippee!" she cried, clapping her hands. "You're going to get married! Maggie's going to be my mother! I'm going to have the nicest, most beautiful mother anybody ever had in the whole world!

"Hey, hey," R.J. laughingly scolded his daughter. "Doesn't your old pa get some of the credit for managing to persuade such a sweet lady to be your mother?"

Nugget giggled and hugged her daddy's neck from behind and planted a kiss on his cheek. "Shoot, Daddy, I knew Maggie would fall for you. I told her so the first day she came to live with us."

R.J. groaned in disbelief while Maggie laughed. "Nugget, you little minx, it's a wonder you didn't scare her straight back to New York," he said.

Nugget kissed her daddy's cheek again for good measure, then slid across the seat to hug Maggie.

"I'm so happy I could shout," Nugget said.

"Then shout," R.J. said, smiling indulgently.

Nugget complied by letting out a squeal that had Maggie covering her ears in response.

"Now I can have brothers and sisters," she burst out with the realization.

"And how many would you like?" R.J. wanted to know.

"Oh, I don't know," she considered seriously. "What do you think, Maggie?"

"Oh, I think about three," Maggie said while her eyes clung to R.J.'s handsome face. "That way there would be four of you—two for me and two for your daddy."

"Yeah!" Nugget exclaimed. Then she asked in after thought, "But what will they be? Boys or girls?"

"Well, what would you like?" Maggie asked.

Nugget's brown eyes grew wide, and she looked at her father. "You mean we can pick out what we want?"

R.J. laughed and reached back and ruffled Nugget's hair. "No, kid, you can't pick out what you want, but we'll try to get what you'd like," he added with a knowing look at Maggie.

As the landscape slipped by, Maggie remembered how ugly Texas had seemed to her when she'd first arrived. Now it was the most beautiful place on earth.

"Who is that at Maggie's house?" Nugget asked as they turned down the gravel road toward home.

Maggie jerked her head around to see a dark sedan parked in front of the old house. She looked at R.J. with a sinking feeling in the pit of her stomach. Had something happened to her parents?

"Were you expecting someone?" R.J. asked.

The question hit her like a sledgehammer because she suddenly realized who it was. "Phillip!" she hissed.

"Phillip?" he repeated warily, his eyes narrowing on her white face.

"When Phillip called, he wanted me to return to New York. I said I wouldn't, and he said if I didn't he would be out here to get me. I . . . I didn't believe him."

By now they had passed Maggie's house and were nearing R.J.'s. He braked the Mustang and pulled into the driveway.

"He must be wanting you pretty badly to fly out after you," R.J. mused rather suspiciously.

Maggie's throat felt as if it were closing off completely, and she clutched her purse to quell the trembling of her hands. "Leon Benetti wants me for a film," she finally managed to whisper.

His head snapped back at her disclosure, and in the back seat Nugget wailed, "But Maggie's not going to be a movie star, she's going ot be my mother!"

"Nugget, go on into the house. I want to talk to Maggie," he told his daughter as he parked the car beneath the shaded carport.

They got out of the Mustang and Maggie watched the child's retreating back as she nervously waited for R.J. to come around to her side of the vehicle.

"Why are you telling me this now?" he demanded, once Nugget was out of earshot.

Maggie unconsciously moistened her lips. "I tried to tell you, but you didn't want to discuss it until we got home," she explained hurriedly.

"My God, Maggie. You knew before we left for Corpus Christi!"

"Yes, I did," she admitted, "but I felt it wasn't important."

"Wasn't important!" he echoed harshly. "What did you plan on doing? Waiting until we had one child in kinder-

garten and the other in diapers, then start crying about how
I cheated you out of being a Hollywood star?''

Maggie studied his face in stunned disbelief. ''You
couldn't love me and ask me that question,'' she accused
''I'm not so foolish that I don't realize that this is my chance
to get in the movies—if I were interested. But I'm not. And
I think I should have the right—''

''The right to keep things from me?''

''It wasn't like that. Besides, you're forgetting it's my ca
reer we're discussing, not yours!''

For long moments he didn't say anything, and Maggie'
heart beat with a sense of dread as his face filled with dis
appointment.

''I thought a relationship, a marriage, meant sharing
Obviously to you it doesn't. You're not the woman
thought you were,'' he stated flatly and turned away from
her.

Maggie scurried around the side of the car to where h
was stabbing the key into the trunk. ''I'm not the sam
woman who first came here! I admit I was a bit spoiled and
selfish, but—''

''You're not the same woman I wanted to marry, either.'
She gasped in shock, but he ignored her response as he be
gan to pull the suitcases out of the trunk. ''I want a woman
who loves me so much she wants to share everything with
me. She wouldn't even consider keeping anything from m
because without me she wouldn't be whole, and in return
wouldn't be complete without her. I just don't think you'r
ready for that kind of commitment, Maggie.'' He slammed
the trunk lid and turned to face her. His features were s
bleak, so dead that Maggie felt ice cold. ''I thought yo
were, but obviously I was wrong.''

''R.J.,'' she pleaded, her hand closing over his forearm
''Give me a chance to—''

He peeled her fingers away from his arm and, for a mo
ment, his hands closed over her small one. The anger wa

gone from his face and voice, but in its place came a sick sort of resignation. "When I asked you to marry me, I told you I'd be willing to leave my home and career for part of the year. I wanted to do the right thing, or at least what I thought was fair. But I thought whatever we decided would be decided together."

He dropped her hand and for a moment his fingers closed about her chin and his amber eyes studied her face as though he was seeing her for the very first time.

"George used to tell me you belonged out here. But he was wrong. We've got a saying here, and it states that you can't live in Texas unless you've got a lot of soul. I think you'd better get your things and go back to your Phillip and your New York and your modeling. You're not ready for this kind of life."

Tears were behind her eyes, pain lanced through her breast, and she marveled that she could still stand here and face him without breaking apart.

"What about Nugget? What do I tell her?" she whispered hoarsely.

"Nothing! I'll take her down to the barn and keep her occupied while you leave."

Maggie couldn't believe his cold, heartless attitude. It was impossible to connect this man with the R.J. she had fallen in love with; it was impossible to believe that suddenly everything was over between them. Is that how love really was—suddenly there, then just as swiftly gone?

"I can't even tell her goodbye?" she cried in total dismay.

"No! It's going to tear her heart out as it is. Let's spare her that much at least."

What about me, R.J., she wanted to scream at him, *what about my heart.* Instead she turned away from him and slowly entered the house to go pack her things.

Since there wasn't anything to steal in Maggie's house, she hadn't bothered to lock it. Apparently Phillip had let himself in, for when she pulled her Alfa Romeo to a stop in front of the house, he burst through the door.

She swiftly climbed out of the car and met him on the brittle grass of the yard.

"What do you mean coming out here, Phillip?" she snapped at him.

He totally ignored her outburst. Instead, he stared at her, his mouth open as his eyes traveled from her hair to her red silk crop top and down to her cream-colored slacks.

"What in God's name have you done to yourself?" he barked, incredulous.

She looked at him, amazed that she was seeing so many things in him that she had never seen before. He was dressed in Italian-cut slacks and an oversize white jacket with a black T-shirt beneath it. He looked so New York, so different from R.J.'s hard, southwestern virility.

"Don't answer my question with a question," she responded angrily. She was full of pain and confusion, and she was also outraged that this man had taken it upon himself to interfere in her life.

"I came out here to get my model, my girl, but I can't believe this—you! Have you gone mad? Your hair is totally ruined, and you look like a blimp!"

Her hands clenched furiously at her sides. "I don't remember asking your opinion."

"Maggie! Benetti is expecting us in two days. There's no way I can take you out there looking like this!"

"I told you, Phillip, I have no intention of going to L.A." She sidestepped him and started toward the house. Everything was already packed in her car. All she had to do now was close up the house and drive away. And she wanted that now; she wanted to get away from Phillip, from R.J. She wanted to leave this place, and everything it had come to mean to her.

Phillip stalked after her and cursed as the screen door slammed in his face. "What are you doing, Maggie—trying to ruin us both?"

She whirled around and faced him as he entered the door. "Phillip, this is it! It's over! You're not pushing me anymore!"

His face hardened with derision. "What have you done? Fallen for some macho cowboy whose main objective in life is to drive around in one of those pickup trucks and spit tobacco juice out the window? Damn," he muttered harshly, "you must have lost what little sense you ever possessed!"

Maggie was blinded with fury and she rushed at him, slapping and clawing his face. His words had snapped her control, and it took Phillip some effort to capture her arms and still her.

"Get out of here! I never want to see you again!" she yelled, managing to pull free of his hold.

Phillip's hand reached up and touched the livid marks on his cheek. "I think you've forgotten you're under contract to me," he said scathingly.

Maggie's laugh was pure mockery. "You've always liked to think you owned me. You've even insinuated to others that we were having an affair. Well, Phillip, you might own the most successful modeling agency in the world, but you're a weak, selfish man. My lawyer will decide where our contract begins and ends!"

Rain drummed against the vinyl roof of the Mustang parked along the curb of the New York City street.

R.J. looked out the windshield and grimaced at the dismal weather. Amarillo was never like this in July and the unaccustomed grayness of the sky depressed him. It was just as well, for depression was a word he'd learned the meaning of these past four weeks. He knew the definition backward and forward, inside and out. He was almost convinced it was his middle name.

He sighed for the umpteenth time and glanced at the gold watch on his wrist. He had been sitting there for almost an hour and a half. Maybe he should go back to the hotel. She might never show up or it might be late at night before she decided to come home. For all he knew, she was out of the country on a modeling stint.

A painful twist hit him somewhere in his middle, and he reached for the door handle. Possibly a fellow tenant could tell him if she was away from the city.

His hand halted just before the latch clicked, and his heart hammered heavily as he spotted a figure striding up the sidewalk on the opposite side of the street. A white skirt fluttered against her legs and her red high heels matched her raincoat. The rain had dampened her hair, but it still bounced in curly tendrils as she walked. There was a sack of groceries in her arms, and he noticed the top of a cornflake box was sticking above the brown paper.

He watched her climb the steps to the brownstone and enter the building. Then she was shutting the door behind her, and the vision was suddenly gone.

The sight of her was anticlimactic, and his fingers gripped the door handle as an uncontrollable quiver rushed through his body. She was so bright, so beautiful, so talented. The whole world was hers for the taking. Why couldn't he have stayed in Amarillo where he belonged? Why couldn't he leave her alone, forget her, let her shine in her own spotlight?

He groaned aloud and looked away from the building. Falling in love with her had hit him hard, and he wondered if he appeared as irrational as he feared he was becoming. These past few weeks all kinds of emotions had assaulted him. Feelings like guilt, selfishness, grief, confusion had tormented him—emotions that had been so foreign to him until he had met her.

He looked back at the brownstone and wished he had the strength to start the Mustang and drive away.

* * *

Maggie tossed her raincoat and heels into the closet and walked barefoot back through the kitchen. She had set the grocery sack on the breakfast bar and now she moved it over to the cabinet and quickly put away the food.

It was a little after six, and she knew she should start preparing something to eat, but she wasn't in the mood for dinner. She had spent most of the afternoon in a coffee shop, and the Danish pastry Mr. Cahill had insisted she eat was still a burning knot in her stomach.

Pushing her wet hair away from her face, she crossed to the stereo, dropped an LP onto the turntable, then poured herself a glass of wine.

The business meeting with Mr. Cahill had been very amicable, but also very involved, and she was exhausted. She curled up on the end of the couch and leaned her head back against the cushions. The wine slid warmly down her throat, and she welcomed its numbing effects. Dallas, Texas. Did she really want to live there? Hadn't Texas done enough to her life already? But on the other hand, the job as a fashion buyer was more appealing than any she had been offered, and Mr. Cahill's idea of bringing high-fashion copies to the middle-class working woman was exactly the kind of thing she would like to do.

Restlessly she rose from the couch and walked over to the windows. The streets were black and shiny with rain and on the sidewalk below, people were dashing about to avoid getting wet. On the stereo Billy Joel was singing "A New York State of Mind," and her lips quirked at the irony.

Her mind was constantly on Amarillo these days, and she thought it was highly unlikely that it was raining there. No, it would be beautiful there, the wide endless sky a hazy blue.

Suddenly the voices were with her again, and even in spite of the music she could hear them clearly. These past weeks her apartment had never been silent. She had kept the radio, the TV, the stereo or something going just to make a noise, to try to drown out the torture in her head. It wasn't working, and she closed her eyes as Nugget's voice insisted on skipping across her mind. *"Put the top down, Daddy, cause me and Maggie want our hair to blow. Come and watch me feed Walter. Maggie, I've caught him a bunch of grasshoppers."* R.J. appeared, his voice slow and distinct. *"Maggie, have you ironed my white shirt? Have you seen those blueprints we were looking over last night? Put that down and come have a beer with me."*

Maggie swallowed more of the wine and blinked the burning moisture from her eyes. She had to take the Dallas job, she frantically concluded. If something didn't happen, didn't change her life from the way it was going now, she was going to go mad with desolation.

A knock on the door penetrated her thoughts, and she crossed the room to answer it.

"Yes, who is it?"

"It's me, Maggie."

For a moment she stared at the door in stunned disbelief. R.J.? R.J.!

"Maggie?"

She took a deep breath and tried to force a detached expression on her face before she opened the door.

Her cool facade came desperately close to crumbling when she faced him. She hadn't forgotten how handsome he was, but it was a shock to be suddenly reminded all over again of his overpowering sensuality. Her legs grew weak in response. He was wearing Levi's, black boots and a white oxford shirt with the sleeves rolled up. Rain glistened on his dark hair and spotted his clothes. He looked so wonderful, so beautifully familiar, that she could do nothing but stand there drinking in the sight of him.

"Are you going to ask me in?"

Numbly she pushed open the door. "Of course."

He stepped into the luxurious surroundings of her apartment, and Maggie motioned him to the couch.

"I was having some wine. Would you like a drink? I don't have any beer, but there's vodka or Scotch."

"Scotch will be fine," he answered as he sank down on the velvet cushions.

Maggie poured the whiskey over a few ice cubes and carried it across to him.

"Thank you," he said, taking the glass from her fingers, and Maggie thought that their formal manner seemed ridiculous after everything that had happened between them.

She took a chair opposite him and did her best to meet his gaze. It was a hard thing to do when her heart insisted on pounding loudly in her ears and her palms were slick with perspiration.

"So," she said, trying to muster a smile. "What brings you to New York? Business?"

He studied her face with a hooded expression. "As a matter of fact, there's a builders' convention going on. I thought it would do me good to attend."

She felt dead inside. "What's the main topic? I thought there wasn't anything about the building business that you didn't already know."

He took a sip of his drink, and Maggie noticed once again how tanned he was and that she ached to touch his skin, to feel it warm and exciting beneath her fingers.

"It's all about solar energy. Many businesses are thinking along those lines, now that utilities are so expensive."

"That should go along with your part of the country quite well. You're certainly not limited on sunshine."

"That's true," he agreed, but he didn't elaborate, and in spite of the music on the stereo, the room seemed unbearably quiet.

Maggie got to her feet and went over to the windows. She wondered why he had called on her. Why couldn't he have attended his convention, then left town?

"How's Nugget?"

"Fine. She's staying over at Helen's."

Maggie sipped her wine, wondering if the child missed her as much as she did Nugget. "How was your flight up here?" she asked, merely to break the tense silence.

When a few moments passed and he didn't answer, she took her eyes off the street to look at him. There was a strange expression on his face, and Maggie's fingers fluttered nervously against the black tie of her blouse.

"I didn't fly up. I drove the Mustang."

She looked at him with incredulity, and he said, "You see, I finally got one of those hang-ups you tried so hard to find in me. I was actually afraid to fly. I was afraid the same thing that happened to James would happen to me and I would never see you again."

She clutched the windowsill behind her. "Me?" she whispered. "I thought you were here for a convention!"

He rose from the couch and went over to her. For the first time, Maggie saw the desperate pain on his face.

"That was a lie. There is no convention." He took a deep breath and raked a hand carelessly through his hair. "I used to pride myself with the fact that I'd never lied to anyone before. But since I met you, that's all I seem to be doing."

Her blue eyes looked into his brown ones, and she found she couldn't quell the sudden trembling of her body. "What are you saying?"

"I'm saying that I've lied to you and myself all along. I lied when I said I didn't want you, I lied when I said it would be easy not to touch you, I lied when I said you didn't have enough soul to live in Texas and that I wanted you to go back to Phillip and New York." He swallowed convulsively, and his hands reached out and curled around her shoulders. "That was the biggest lie of all."

His touch broke her composure, and she crumpled against his chest, hot, heavy sobs wrenching her body. "Oh, R.J. I've been sick without you! I hate it here. I hate living alone, I hate not being with you and Nugget."

His arms crushed her close, and his head bent so that his face was meshed within her damp hair. "Maggie, can you forgive me? Can you believe me when I tell you I was filled with jealousy and fear when we arrived home from Corpus Christi and found your agent there?"

She lifted her tear-drenched face in order to look at him. "Fear? You've probably never feared anything in your life. And now you've said the word twice within the past five minutes."

His mouth twisted ruefully. "It seems you've acquainted me with lots of feelings I'd never experienced before. But from the first time I met you, I was afraid of becoming involved with you, afraid of loving you, afraid of not being man enough to hold a woman like you. Then when I found out you didn't tell me about the Benetti deal, I felt like you had deliberately tried to exclude me from your life. It hurt, hurt like hell, Maggie!"

She shook her head, unable to believe he was saying these things. An hour ago she thought her life was over, that she would never see him again. "You'll never know what it did to me when you sent me away," she said.

His face filled with regret. "I was crazy to send you away. I realized that a few hours after you'd left, and I'd had the chance to cool off. But then I tried to tell myself you were better off without Nugget and me holding you back. This past month I've come to learn that love is a very selfish emotion; I want you to be my wife, even if it ruins your career."

Suddenly Maggie began to laugh and smother his face with kisses. "I don't have a career anymore, R.J. There's no more Phillip, no modeling, no film deal, just a job offer in Dallas that I desperately want to refuse. All I want is you, Nugget, and those three babies we talked about. I want Walter and the horses, the wind and dust, and every other damned thing Amarillo has to offer."

He laughed with sheer exuberance and kissed her lips until they were both breathless and trembling.

"I think I should warn you that the family has grown since you left," he said with a grin.

Her eyebrows arched in response to his words. "Really? How do you mean?" she whispered, her mind swimming dizzily with love for him.

"Nugget was so distraught over your leaving that I let her have an armadillo and a cockatoo."

"Good for Nugget," she murmured. "Maybe she can give me some advice when I need to convince you of something."

He laughed as Maggie's hands moved tenderly over the warm strength of his chest. "You know, George did know what he was talking about. You *do* belong in Texas, right by my side."

Maggie didn't waste time telling him she had known that long ago.

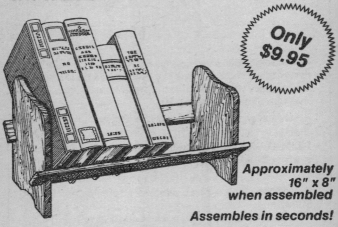

Silhouette Intimate Moments

MARCH MADNESS!

Get Intimate with
Four Very Special Authors

Silhouette Intimate Moments has chosen March as the month to launch the careers of three new authors—Marilyn Pappano, Paula Detmer Riggs and Sibylle Garrett—and to welcome top-selling historical romance author Nancy Morse to the world of contemporary romance.

For years Silhouette Intimate Moments has brought you the biggest names in romance. Join us now and let four exciting new talents take you from the desert of New Mexico to the backlots of Hollywood, from an Indian reservation in South Dakota to the Khyber Pass of Afghanistan.

Coming in March from Silhouette Intimate Moments:

SACRED PLACES: Nancy Morse
WITHIN REACH: Marilyn Pappano
BEAUTIFUL DREAMER: Paula Detmer Riggs
SEPTEMBER RAINBOW: Sibylle Garrett

Silhouette Intimate Moments, this month and every month.
Available wherever paperback books are sold.

IM-MM

You won't want to miss a single one of the heart-felt stories presented by Silhouette Special Edition; and when you take advantage of this special offer, you won't have to.

You'll also receive a FREE subscription to the Silhouette Books Newsletter as long as you remain a member. Each lively issue is filled with news on upcoming titles, interviews with your favorite authors, even their favorite recipes.

To become a home subscriber and receive your first 4 books FREE, fill out and mail the coupon today!

Silhouette Special Edition®